What reviewers have to say a̶l̶

"Talented author Marjorie Grace Patricia Bridget Owen offers an original plot with an interesting cast of characters you will enjoy meeting. Their private agendas may get in the road of the investigation, but they certainly add a flavor to the story which is a comfortable blend of mystery and romance as lived by very likable ordinary people.

Recommended as a pleasant read for any mystery buff who doesn't like car chases or shoot 'em ups. I think Agatha C. would like this one. I did." - Mystery Fiction

"Ms. Owen weaves a tale of suspense that keeps you hanging. Richard will pull out all the stops to find the truth and suspecting a trusted official will be the least of his problems. The connection between Mrs. Clayton and the murderer is one that is very surprising. I had no idea who committed the crime. This one will leave you guessing until the very end." - Coffee Time Romance Reviews

Majorie Grace Patricia Bridget Owen

Ladies of Class

A Richard Hayward Murder Mystery

Marjorie Grace Patricia Bridget Owen

ISBN: 978-0-9793327-5-3

PUBLISHED BY VINTAGE ROMANCE PUBLISHING, LLC
www.vrpublishing.com

Dedication

Marjorie was an avid reader. She spent many hours at her local library in Burgess Hill, West Sussex, England. The 'Ladies' of the library knew Marjorie well. They would find books, save them, and let her know when titles of interest would arrive. Marjorie read many murder mysteries, detective, and suspense stories.

In her later years, Marjorie lived in an 'assisted living' community. She had her own apartment and was a very private person. Even though the facility had many activities for the residents, Marjorie rarely took part. She would much prefer to go to the library, collect more books, and sit by the large picture window overlooking the gardens and read. This may be where she did some of her writing.

There is no indication of time frame as to when she did write her books and stories. However, we surmise that her writings were done over many years. Marjorie had one good friend, Jackie, who she had known for many years. Jackie would bring her books, papers, shop for her, and visit frequently.

So to the local library in Burgess Hill, to Jackie, and all those who loved Marjorie, we dedicate this book!

Majorie Grace Patricia Bridget Owen

Introduction by Dee Owen

Marjorie Owen, or "Mum" as I called my mother-in-law, told her son, Mike that she had written a couple of stories and let him read them some years ago. She expressed no interest in having them published at that time. He was never aware of the amount that she had written until she passed away.

Mike, being an only child and having no aunts or uncles, is the sole heir to Marjorie's estate. He discovered the box full of Mum's writings on clearing her flat in England and took them back to the USA.

As an avid reader, I became fascinated with Mum's stories and books. All her writings were handwritten on legal size paper or note books and on both sides of the paper. I began reading some of the short stories (there are fifty plus).

I was soon hooked and decided to attempt the monumental task of transcribing them to computer. Mum's writing was not the easiest to read, however, but I had myself the challenge and was going to follow through.

At first, Mike assisted me with the 'translation' of Mum's hand writing. At times, we both became frustrated with each other and Mum, but after a couple of stories, I became an expert at reading Mum's writing and even improved my own typing skills and speed.

As yet, I have not yet completed the task even after three years of work. With a few more stories to go and two novels to transcribe, I decided to see if my opinion about Mum's writing skills were correct and began submitting several of the short stories for publishing.

Several of Mum's stories were accepted for publishing by online magazines and were published without pay. But exposure is important. A small success spurred me to try for bigger things.

That's where "Ladies of Class" comes in. This first book of Mum's is to be published in March 2008. Mike and I are really happy and hope that the book will be a success and lead to further publication of Mum's writings.

To find out more about her writings and her life, visit our blog at http://marjo-mumswriting.blogspot.com or our website which is http://pangirl.tripod.com.

Chapter One

Laura Clayton's last day on earth was as ordinary as any other, right up to the few moments before she came to her messy end.

The only unusual thing about it was that she awoke to brilliant sunshine dancing on the bedroom window. March had been a spiteful month, not only coming like a lion but roaring its way through with no let up in the constant rain and lashing gales. It seemed to have no intention of going out like a lamb, but on this Saturday, the 31st, it finally relented.

"I don't believe it!" Laura said aloud, scrambling into a housecoat and hurrying to look out at the phenomenon. But it was true and everything in the garden, which yesterday had looked dreary and sullen, was nodding and smiling and perking up in the unaccustomed brightness and warmth.

Laura was a happy person and, being a countrywoman at heart, was never too affected by changes in the weather, but she loved her garden. As always, her eyes, after the first quick look around, came to rest on the flowering cherry tree. She thought how much the buds would be enjoying the sun and pictured in imagination its glory when in full bloom.

When her husband died five years previously, all Laura's friends expected she would sell the house with its large garden and move into something smaller. She fobbed them off with vague promises to consider it.

To her son, Alec, she said, "they'd think I was mad if I

told them I couldn't bear to leave my lovely cherry tree, but that is the truth. I think it'd miss me if I went away." Alec wasn't too sure if he understood his mother, either, but his young wife said it made sense to her. So being outnumbered by his women folk, he wisely held his tongue.

Laura, bathed and dressed, went to the kitchen, picking two letters off the mat as she went. Looking at the handwriting with pleasure, she left them unopened until she was sitting down to her coffee, toast, and marmalade.

One letter from Alec was short but the other, although reasonably brief, caused her to exclaim with surprise and to need another reading to grasp it. She was just coming to the end of it for the second time when the sound of the side gate closing dragged her thoughts away. A glance at the kitchen clock showed her it was later than she'd thought, and here was Milly to prove it.

Milly Patcham, born a cockney and still with the dialect to prove it, opened the kitchen door and bustled in, talking as usual. She always began the conversation half way down the path, and Laura never knew what the beginning of the sentence was. In fact, sometimes it took her quite a while to guess what the topic of conversation might be.

Thirty years of Milly's ministrations had given both women a respect and affection for the other and, allowing for a difference in upbringing, they could honestly look on each other as friends.

"—said to 'im 'e ought to look after 'er better. No business to be luggin' them 'eavy bags about, and so I told 'er, too."

"Whom are we talking about this time?" Laura asked

in a resigned tone.

"Bert the milkman, acourse. Yer know 'is wife's due any day. Two misses she's 'ad already, and she didn't ought to be takin' any chances. Saw 'er in the supermarket yesterday. You've been lucky this time, I said. Don't push yer luck. If yer doesn't watch out, you'll be 'avin one o' those mongrels!"

"Mongols not mongrels," Laura corrected her patiently. "What a cheerful thing to say to the poor girl. Anyway, I saw her myself a day or two back, and she looks perfectly well to me."

"That's as may be, madam dear. But you read some funny things in the papers. Never 'eard about all this when I was young—must be all to do with this population explosion I shouldn't wonder."

Laura smothered a laugh and stored this new 'Millyism' in her memory to tell Alec.

"Sit down and have a cup of coffee before you start work. Forget all the gloom and misery. I've had a piece of good news in the post this morning—well, two in fact—but the most important is that Alec's coming tomorrow."

"Oh that'll be nice, madam dear. Is 'e bringing the wife and baby? 'Ow long are they staying?"

"Only Alec and just a flying visit. He's going abroad on Monday for the firm, starting early, so thought he'd break his journey here and stay the night."

"Bet you're pleased about that. It'll be like old times to 'ave Alec all to yourself, won't it?"

"Milly! You'll make me feel guilty saying things like that," Laura protested. "I love my daughter-in-law dearly as you well know. But yes, I've got to admit it'll be lovely to have him on his own. Anyway, I've got a little problem I want to discuss."

Milly's eyes lit up with avid curiosity, and Laura could have kicked herself. Milly was a treasure beyond price and as loyal as they came, but she was an inveterate gossip. If anyone had accused her of being a mischief-maker, she would have been scandalized, but there was no doubt about it—her unruly tongue had caused more than one bit of bother in the town. Everyone knew Milly, and Milly knew everyone.

Wisely, Laura made no comment but said briskly, "come on, drink up. We've got work to do—blankets and sheets to get out for Alec's bed. I'd like his room ready before I go out. I've a full day ahead and dinner with the vicar tonight, so there won't be much time."

That got Milly moving and for the next couple of hours, the two women worked companionably together until Laura glanced at her watch.

"I'll have to be off. Hairdressing appointment. Will you finish up by yourself?"

"Acourse, madam dear. Now, does yer want me to leave anything for yer lunch?"

"No, thanks. I'll probably get a bite at that new café on the High Street. Then I'll finish the shopping, get a bottle of Scotch for Alec, too. Pity I don't like it, or there would have been some in the house."

Hurriedly she changed her skirt and top, threw on a raincoat, and went down into the white-painted hall.

"'Ang on a tick! It's turned cloudy. Yer needs an 'ead scarf, 'specially if you're going to the 'airdressers. I put one in the 'all drawer the other day."

She rummaged about while Laura waited impatiently. In her haste, she pulled the whole drawer out, scattering the contents on the carpet, amongst them a small dog collar.

"Oh, blast!" she said, quickly trying to shuffle it out of sight, but Laura had seen and the tears came into her eyes. She picked the little collar up, stroked it affectionately, sighed, and put it back in the drawer.

"It's no good. I'll have to get another dog. When old Sammy died, I swore never again, but I do miss him about the place."

"Now, madam dear! You know you said you wouldn't, and when young Alec was 'ere, 'e told me not to encourage you if you started talkin' about one. You nearly break yer 'eart and make yerself ill when they die. Don't do it."

Laura snuffled and blew her nose. Looking at Milly's anxious face, she gave a watery smile. "I'm an old fool, aren't I? But as a matter of fact, I've already broken the news to Alec that I'm thinking of having another. So far he's made no comment, but I expect I'll get round him. Goodness! Look at the time. I must fly. I'll see you on Monday."

Milly wasn't to know it was the last time she'd ever see the woman whom she'd learned to love and respect.

* * * *

Later on, when it became vitally important to work out Laura's subsequent movements, it was the easiest job imaginable. Practically every minute could be accounted for—she was so well known. More to the point, there was barely a minute when she was alone, even taking a neighbour in while she was dressing for her dinner with the vicar, in order to complete plans for the next Women's Institute sale of work.

Laura lived in the oldest and nicest part of the town; the heart of what had been a village when she came to it as a bride more than forty years ago. But the tentacles of progress had stretched out greedily, snapping up farms, meadows and woods, spawning streets of Council houses, a factory estate, and a shopping complex. Swamping the charm and character Burshill once possessed.

Her house was in one of four roads surrounding the original village green, now a more formalized park, with a covered-in swimming pool, children's playground, and made-up paths. But most of the trees had been left, and cricket was still played in summer. The neighbouring houses had maintained their standards, and although Laura was saddened by all the changes, she still loved her house...and her cherry tree.

The Vicarage, to which she was headed for her dinner engagement, was diagonally opposite on the further side of the green, standing beside the parish church, half empty these days. The Reverend George Amberley and his wife, Julia, were old friends, and the five minute walk across the grass was a two-way passage in constant use from both houses. This evening, mindful of her long skirt and high-heeled shoes, Laura kept to the paths, her W.I. companion walking with her as far as the Vicarage gates where she said goodbye.

Julia Amberley opened the door before she knocked and greeted her affectionately. George's melancholy face peered out from a door to the right of the hall.

"Hullo!" Laura said cheerfully at the sight of his woebegone visage. "And what's the matter with you this time?"

Julia laughed. "How well you know my dear old hypochondriac. But he really had got something to worry about tonight—a bit of bronchitis rattling around, and he's afraid it'll keep him out of the pulpit tomorrow. As if it would! I'd be expected to produce a death certificate if George didn't turn up on the dot."

George gave the two smiling women a reproachful look. "It's nothing to joke about, my dear. I ought to be in bed resting for my big day. You know the Bishop's coming for the evening service. I don't want to be croaking away in his presence."

"Good thing Laura knows you. Otherwise she'd be feeling most unwelcome. If you want to go to bed, go. We shan't miss you."

With a martyred air, George refused. "I wouldn't dream of doing such a thing when we have a guest in the house."

"Come now," Laura rallied him. "I'm one of your oldest friends, and I shan't mind in the least. You know how beastly your attacks of bronchitis can get. I'd hate to have it on my conscience if your voice deserted you for the all-important service tomorrow. Please go to bed to oblige me."

George was finally persuaded and took himself off upstairs. By doing so, he helped to forge the last link in poor Laura's destiny. For this he'd never forgive himself.

After the two women had eaten and Julia nipped up to peep at the invalid—"sleeping like a baby," she reported—they settled down by the fire, heavy curtains drawn against the chill March night, for a comfortable gossip.

"I hope we'll see you in church tomorrow evening. Help to swell the congregation a bit and impress the Bishop."

Laura was apologetic. "I'm afraid not. Alec's coming on a flying visit." She explained the circumstances, adding, "So you see, I'd like to spend the evening with him. We'll have a lot to talk about." She said nothing about the special topic she wanted his advice on. This led to a cozy chat about their respective families, and time passed quickly.

At ten o'clock Laura said she'd be on her way, knowing her friend would want to attend to George's needs for the night. When Julia opened the door to let her out, she uttered an exclamation. "Good grief! Look at that!"

To their equal surprise, a dense fog surrounded them, thick and impenetrable as a London pea-souper. Totally unexpected.

"Must have been all that glorious sun we've had today," Laura commented. The lunchtime cloud had soon gone away.

"You can't go home in this. It's horrible. Oh, why on earth did George have to get his rotten bronchitis tonight? He'd have escorted you back."

"Stop clucking. It's only a five-minute walk away, for goodness sake. I'm a big girl now and not likely to get lost."

Julia wasn't happy about it, but Laura insisted; she went off with a cheery "goodnight," and was immediately swallowed up in the fog. She kept to the paths which were as familiar to her as her own garden, but she found the silence more eerie than she would have imagined. Even distant traffic noises were hushed, and she felt completely isolated in a strange world. She pushed doggedly on and, without any trouble, found herself turning onto the path, lined with tall trees, which would lead her out almost opposite her own house.

Suddenly, surprisingly, a figure stepped out from behind one of the great horse-chestnuts and stood in front of her. Laura wasn't of a nervous disposition, but she was startled. Then, coming face to face with the apparition, she recognized it.

"Oh, it's you!" said Laura.

Chapter Two

Detective Chief Inspector Richard Hayward missed with the hammer, hitting his thumb instead. He cursed with bitterness and fluency, his face a peculiar greenish-white with temper, extreme fatigue, and pain.

The little lady kneeling on the floor unpacking books from a crate looked up at her tall son sharply. She rose to her feet, saying briskly, "That's enough, now!"

"Sorry, Mother," he apologized mechanically, but he allowed her to take the hammer from his unresisting hand.

"I'm not talking about your swearing," tartly. "Goodness knows I should be used to it after all these years—and your father's before you. What I mean is you've done enough for today. Moving house is an awful job at the best of times, but with you convalescing and starting back to work on Monday—far too soon in my opinion—" her voice trailed off as she noticed his drawn face. "Sit down, for heaven's sake. Would you like a cup of tea before you go to bed? You're not getting anything stronger. And you're taking a sleeping pill. No arguing."

Richard grinned, and Ella was thankful to see the old familiar twinkle back in his eyes. "Stop treating me like a five-year old. I've been away from home a long time now. I'm a grown up married man."

"But your wife's in New Zealand, and you're recovering from a broken bone and moving all at the same time, so somebody's got to look after you. Men! Haven't got the sense of a five-year old. Sit!"

Obediently, he sat. While Ella clattered about in the kitchen making the tea, she saw Richard staring despairingly at the chaos in his new living room. It was the first time he'd experienced a home removal. Ella saw the disgruntled look on his face, perhaps wondering if it would ever be straight. She wondered why on earth his darling Kate had fallen in love with this funny old place and then rushed off to New Zealand before she could organize the move?

Of course she had to go, Ella thought loyally. When the phone call came to say Kate's father had suffered a stroke and might not recover, there was no option. For this reason, Richard had forbidden Ella to let Kate know about his own accident.

She understood that Richard hadn't wanted his wife to make the agonizing decision of where her priorities lay, especially as her father seemed to be making a wonderful recovery.

Richard was half asleep when Ella returned with a tray, but he sat up and sipped his tea, giving her a grateful look. The drink seemed to revive him as he glanced around.

"This really is a strange sort of house, isn't it? Hope to God Kate likes it after all."

"Of course, she will, and I think it's lovely. Most original, too. It's got definite possibilities, and with Kate's artistic leanings, I should say she'll make it a showplace in no time at all."

The house had started life in Queen Anne's day as two labourers' cottages then knocked into one by some unknown owner. Built on a hill, it was on two levels, with an unexpected step down in the middle of the living room floor. This was one long room with a fireplace at each end and behind it, a minute kitchen and a door into the back garden. That was all.

Then a narrow staircase led to the second floor, again, with a step in the middle, which made for a division between bedroom and bathroom. The staircase continued to yet a third floor where there were two more rooms. In all, a long, narrow house and certainly not everybody's vision of the ideal home. But Kate adored it, and Ella knew her daughter-in-law was looking forward to pottering around in junk shops and auction rooms finding the appropriate bits and bobs she wanted to suit the decor.

"I wish to God she'd hurry up and come home," Richard burst out passionately.

Ella trod warily. She'd had a nasty feeling for the past week or so that Richard was worrying about Kate, but she didn't know why. She was very fond of her daughter-in-law but was beginning to think it was high time she returned. She did a little gentle probing.

"Does she say anything about it? I know you had a letter yesterday. Is her father still keeping up his good progress?"

Richard was a very private person and a proud one. Normally, he would never have dreamed of voicing his innermost feelings, but tonight, his tiredness, the nagging ache in his leg, the day's strain, broke his defenses.

"I don't know, Mum, and that's the truth." (He hadn't called her 'mum' for years!) "I'm beginning to wonder if she wants to come back at all. You know what doubts she had about marrying me and staying in England...I thought she was contented enough after two years of it, but maybe going back has unsettled her."

"Bloody nonsense!" The vehemence of the swear

word obviously surprised her son. "You've always been a daft beggar where Kate's concerned. Chock-full of arrogance and self-confidence where anything else is involved but never been able to believe she loves you, have you? Why, you silly imbecile, the girl's besotted about you, and everyone knows it but you. Stop talking such rubbish, or I shall lose all patience!"

The verbal spanking cheered Richard up a bit, but he wasn't quite convinced. "It's her letters, you see. They've been getting shorter and shorter, and they haven't...well, they aren't as affectionate as they used to be. I've just got this feeling something's wrong, but I can't put a finger on it."

"I'll lay a finger on you if you carry on like this, Detective Chief Inspector. You're a bit under par with your stay in the hospital and all that trouble. You always were a rotten patient, and now, you're just feeling sorry for yourself. Stop it! Now take this sleeping tablet, go to bed, and in the morning, you'll kick yourself for being such a wet!"

Richard's brows lowered. He swallowed the pill of his mother's verbal direction without his customary argument, but when they both stood up, he gave his mother a bear-hug. No further words were necessary between them on the subject, and he looked obscurely comforted.

Ella smacked his behind and said, "Leave the tray. I'll just rinse the cups, and everything else can wait till tomorrow."

She drew back the curtains. "Good Lord! Look at that fog. Hope it means another sunny day tomorrow. Now off to bed and don't forget to say 'Rabbits.' First of April in the morning. In fact,", looking at the clock, "it's almost that now."

Richard disappeared upstairs to the bathroom, Ella to the kitchen. While she was washing the crocks and tidying generally, a slight frown marred her usually placid face. She was recollecting the recent conversation, dismissed out of hand Richard's gloomy forebodings. Of course Kate would return sooner or later but better sooner than later.

For a moment, she even considered writing to the girl herself to delicately hint that Richard was missing her; but she shook her head reprovingly. "Don't be an interfering old bag," she admonished herself. "They must sort out their own problems."

Pity, though, that his first few weeks in Burshill should have begun under such inauspicious conditions. She was tremendously proud of her son, although, wild horses wouldn't have dragged such an admission out of her.

Following his father's footsteps in the Police Force, Richard's advancement had been nothing short of spectacular. It was generally believed he was the youngest officer ever to have achieved his recent promotion to the rank of Detective Chief Inspector and with his promotion, had come Richard's transfer to Burshill.

Ella was sure that Richard was pleased with the move, mainly to get away from the local Press. He'd had a small string of successes, culminating in his single-handed apprehension of an armed villain, and reporters were beginning to follow his progress with more attention than he liked.

Kate had told Ella of the occasion when he really lost his cool and nearly threw one importunate representative from the local rag out on his ear.

"Look here!" He'd raged. "Stop trying to make me some sort of Peter Wimsey and Lew Archer rolled into one. I'm not a bloody fictional private eye. Detection these days is mostly commonsense and a scrap of psychology, and a helluva lot of hard work from foot-slogging bobbies. You chaps watch too much television. Real life is nothing like it."

So he'd come to Burshill, but, of course, his reputation had preceded him. There was a certain amount of antagonism to overcome—human nature being what it is—but Ella had no doubt he'd cope. In a way, he'd become a bit more human to his fellows when he'd broken the bone in his leg, not from some heroic deed but slipping on a patch of hidden ice! She smiled at the thought of his discomfiture over that episode, hung the tea towel up to dry, switched off the kitchen light, and prepared for her own exit bedwards.

At that moment, the telephone bell rang. Ella nearly jumped out of her skin. By official request, the phone had been left from the previous owners, so probably this late call was from some friend who didn't know of the change of an occupier. Curiously, she picked it up.

"Hullo?"

A man's voice asked if she was Mrs. Hayward.

"Mrs. Hayward, senior," she stated."Good evening, madam. May I speak to the Chief Inspector, please?"

Ella was a copper's widow and a copper's mother, but at this moment, the mother came uppermost. "He's in bed asleep," she lied.

The voice at the other end was polite but firm. "I'm so sorry, Mrs. Hayward, but I'm afraid I must insist. This is urgent."

Ella felt like telling him to go to hell, but she considered she might be fighting a losing battle. "Who are you?" she asked crossly.

"Detective Sergeant Findon from Burshill Police. Your son will know me."

By this time, Richard was at the top of the stairs in his pajamas. "What's going on?"

"A Detective Findon or somebody insisting on a word with you. I told him you were asleep."

Richard frowned but came downstairs and took the phone from his mother's hand.

* * * *

"Hayward here. What's the trouble?"

"I'm really sorry to drag you out of bed, sir, but the Chief Constable wants to see you."

Richard's eyes widened. "What now?" He glanced at his watch. "It's past midnight. Look here. Is this some kind of April Fool's Day joke?"

Findon retorted, his voice a combination of shock and anger. "It most certainly is not, sir!"

A more human note crept into his voice. "I almost wish it was! Anyway, sir, my orders are to send a car for you right away. Sir John is at home and would like you to meet him there. Allowing for this perishing fog, the driver should be with you in about ten minutes."

Ella fidgeted about beside him. "Surely you're not going out now!" she remonstrated.

"Afraid I've got no option, luv. The Chief Constable himself wants me right away, so it must be something important. While I throw a few clothes on, will you be a dear and make me a strong black coffee? That blasted sleeping pill of yours is starting to work, and I need my wits about me."

* * * *

Richard dressed in a thick sweater and denims—perhaps a subconscious desire to ram it home to the Chief Constable that he was still on official sick leave. But before he'd had time to take more than a few sips of the scalding coffee, the police car was at the door. The fog, he noticed with relief, was much less dense. The driver introduced himself, and they were off to Sir John Bury's residence, which was about ten miles outside the town.

"Any idea what this is about?" Richard asked.

"We've had a murder tonight, sir. A Mrs. Laura Clayton—very nice lady indeed. We all knew and liked her. She did a lot of good in the town."

"And Sir John's interest...?"

"Well, sir, I'm sure he'd rather tell you about it himself. But he and the murdered lady had been friends for years. He's pretty cut up about it, and he'll be on our backs—if you'll pardon me, sir—until this gets cleared up."

The road dipped into a hollow where the fog still lingered quite thickly. The driver concentrated on his careful maneuvering, and Richard relapsed into silence, fighting the sleepiness which was threatening to overcome him. Trust this to happen on one of the few occasions that he'd ever taken a sleeping tablet!

Chapter Three

Sir John Bury's house was large and imposing like the man himself. Richard had met him once on some previous occasion but knew little about him. Sir John flung the front door open before the car stopped and came out onto the wide front steps. The two men evaluated each other and both seemed to approve of what they saw.

Tonight, neither Sir John nor Richard were their normal selves. There was a strong sense of mingled sorrow and anger enveloping the Chief Constable. But apparently, he wasn't too immersed in his own troubles to notice Richard's exhaustion.

"Come in, my boy. We'll go into my study; there's a good fire to warm you. Would you like a cup of tea or something stronger if you fancy it? Good of you to turn out. How's the leg?"

The study was essentially a man's room—leather-covered chairs, masses of books, and mementos everywhere of Sir John's military career. Richard envied the possessor and thought, fleetingly, of his own 'funny little place.' He refused a drink and asked Sir John to tell him what had happened.

The older man's face clouded over; there was no doubt he'd had an overwhelming shock. Briefly and succinctly, he gave the details. Laura Clayton's body had been discovered in the park, only a few feet away from her own home.

"I won't go into medical details. You'll get those tomorrow, but from a preliminary report, the doctor says it's a wonder the finder didn't stumble across the murderer also. It was that close to the deed."

"Who found her, sir?"

"Oddly enough, her own milkman. He was taking his wife home from a visit to his mother's. Bert somebody is his name. He recognized Laura immediately, but with the thick fog, he didn't see anything else. And, of course, there was another complication."

"Yes, sir?"

"Bert's wife was expecting a baby. She's had two miscarriages up to now, and as soon as she saw the body and the blood—although there was little of the latter— she had screaming hysterics and promptly started her labour pains. As you can imagine, we got precious little out of the milkman! He was in a fine old quandary, a dead body at his feet and his wife beginning to have a baby. Not to mention the fog and nobody around."

"What on earth did he do?"

"Shouted like mad—he's got a roar like a bull—and a couple of fellows on their way home from the pub heard him. One rushed to the nearest house to phone, and the law took over from there. Trouble is we can get nothing out of Bert whoever-he-is at the moment. Seems it's touch and go with the wife and/or the baby, and he's nearly demented with worry. Understandable, I suppose, but damn inconvenient."

The warmth from the fire was making Richard feel worse by the minute. Taking the bull by the horns, he interrupted Sir John's narrative.

"I wonder, sir, if I might ask for a cup of black coffee. I'm not feeling too bright at present, and I want a clear head for the rest of the story."

Sir John stared at him in open astonishment.

Normally he would ring the bell for the servant or his wife would deal with the request.

Flustered, he said, "Of course, of course. Tell you what, we'll get your driver in, and he can make coffee for all of us. Daresay he'll be glad of a cup, too. My wife's away, or she'd do it like a shot."

He bustled out and, in a short while, the police driver was heard in the kitchen making the coffee.

"Now, sir," Richard resumed. "Any ideas about this murder? I understand you knew the lady well."

The sadness in the Chief Constable's eyes was apparent. "Known her since we were both young," he said gruffly. "In fact, there was a time when...oh, well, all water under the bridge now. We both made happy marriages, and all four of us were the best of friends. But who would want to kill her, I can't imagine. She hadn't an enemy in the world."

"I know, I know! Everybody says that when there's a murder, but, in Laura's case, it's literally true. Ask anyone."

"It's also literally true that she was murdered, sir. If she had no personal enemies, it must have been just the random killing— a mugging, for example."

Sir John looked thoughtful. "Don't want to teach you your business, Hayward, but some instinct makes that idea stick in my gullet. You're new here, but you must have seen already how low our crime rate is. Rising a bit now with the influx of newcomers while the town's still expanding, but it's all petty stuff still. A few break-ins, a bit of Saturday domestic trouble when the old man's had a skinful, but never any real violence. A few young thugs, of course, but they make their way to the big seaside town a few miles away; don't come back till the last train leaves, either. We've got a good dossier on the known troublemakers and, believe me, they'll be looked at."

He paused for thought then went on. "Laura's handbag was beside her on the path. Muggers don't usually murder. They snatch and run. But her jewelry was all there."

"But if he'd heard this Bert and his wife coming, mightn't he have panicked and run?"

"Could be, I suppose," Sir John agreed doubtfully, "but surely he'd have grabbed her bag which was easily accessible? And there's one more thing. Unless he had the devil's own luck, he made a thoroughly professional job of the actual stabbing, our doctor said. Knew exactly where to strike."

Richard's head felt full of cotton-wool. They seemed to be going round in circles. He searched Sir John's worried face. There was no doubt the old boy was genuinely 'cut up' as the police driver had so graphically described it. He shook his head to try and clear it and took a deep draught of the obnoxious brew the driver called coffee. Probably only used to the instant variety, he thought uncharitably.

"Seems we're in a bit of a hole then, doesn't it, sir? You say the lady hadn't an enemy in the world; you don't think any of the local talent's responsible. Who does it leave?"

Sir John sighed wearily. "That's what I want you to find out, Hayward. It's unethical of me to say such a thing, but I want you to let everything else go until the bastard's caught. By God! I want that more than anything else in the world."

"Go to her house tomorrow, run through all her things, and see the milkman and Milly Patcham, her daily

woman. Oh, and her son, Alec, will be arriving tomorrow.
I've been trying to raise him on the phone but no luck. So
let him have tonight in peace. Milly's in a state of shock,
but she told me Alec's expected sometime in the
morning."

He pulled himself together and glanced at Richard
apologetically. "You don't need me to tell you who to see
and what to do. You come to us with a reputation for
'getting your man'. That's why I routed you out of bed
and why I hope you'll be willing to set the ball rolling first
thing in the morning. I know you aren't officially due in
until Monday, but this is a personal favour I'm asking."

Silently, Richard cursed his 'reputation'. And talk
about setting the ball rolling in the morning. Didn't the
man see by the carriage clock on his mantelpiece that it
was nearly 2:00 a.m.? He couldn't think of any more
questions to ask and hoped to God he'd be allowed to get
away now. Bed had never seemed more inviting—well,
perhaps that wasn't strictly true, he thought with a
private smile.

But the Chief Constable seemed oblivious to the
hour. He was really wound up. Richard, half asleep, let
the monologue swish about his bemused head. Sir John
was talking of Laura and such phrases as 'a beautiful girl',
'full of fun', and 'so good to my wife', etc., rolled into the
over warm room.

Eventually, the man ran out of steam. Richard was
seen off the premises together with the driver, who was
manfully trying to suppress his yawns.

As the car was about to draw away, Sir John had one
last contribution. "Now, don't forget. I want to be kept
fully informed of everything you find out. Don't hesitate
to ring me at any hour of the day or night."

"Wonder if he ever goes to bed!" the driver muttered rebelliously. Richard was too tired to reprimand him.

When he reached home, his mother came downstairs in her dressing gown, took one look at his face, and after kissing him goodnight, retired again without a word.

Richard dropped his clothes on the floor, fell into bed, and was as dead to the world as if he'd been pole-axed.

* * * *

Surprisingly, after such a short night's sleep, Richard awoke refreshed, whistling in the bathroom. He called down to his mother that he could eat anything except a horse for his breakfast. Within a few minutes, he could hear her bustling about in the kitchen.

After breakfast, he told his mother the Chief Constable's story but wasn't very sanguine about his chances of finding the killer. "To hear him talk, this lady would seem to have been a combination of Helen of Troy, Florence Nightingale, and Joan of Arc. Unless one of her friends did her in out of jealousy of all this beauty and goodness, I still think it was a random killing. It's all right for the C.C to think this is a town filled with angels, but drugs, aren't unknown here. Maybe some punk high on glue or angel-dust or whatever didn't stop to ask how many times she went to church before he clobbered her!"

"Richard! You sound so callous when you talk like that. There are still a few decent people, you know."

"Sorry, Mother, but if you'd had to listen nonstop for what seemed like hours to this lady's catalogue of virtues, you'd be a bit cheesed off."

In spite of the levity, Richard was already considering the first moves. As his mother had said, there were a few decent people left, and he wasn't having one in his manor taken off like that without doing his damndest to nail the villain. He wasn't hopeful; he had no ideas. He was hoping he'd feel differently by the end of the day.

"Do you want the last piece of toast?" he asked, taking it without waiting for an answer.

"My goodness! - You're a bit bobbish today!" His mother seemed delighted. "What a change from yesterday."

"Don't remind me..." Richard broke off, toast half way to his mouth, gazing round in astonishment. "Talk about a difference! When did you do all this, for God's sake?"

The books were in their cases, pictures on the walls, furniture in place; it was beginning to look like a home.

"Some of it last night after you went out; I knew I shouldn't sleep until you were back. And some of us get up early in the morning!"

"Unkind!" Richard mourned. "And me a poor invalid, too. But thanks a lot, you treasure among women. I'm afraid I'm not going to be much help today either. When the Lord High Muck-a-Muck says 'jump', we all jump."

Richard could drive only short distances and, as the police station was only a few miles off, he thankfully got behind the wheel of the Volkswagen and left home. After arriving in his office, he noticed he seemed to be expected. *The bush telegraph does well in this parish.*

With a grumble, he asked for all the paper work so far available on the Laura Clayton murder. There was quite a considerable pile, considering how short a time had elapsed.

"Somebody's been burning the midnight oil, by the look of it," he said to the Station Sergeant. That gentleman raised eyes and hands to heaven without need for comment.

"By the way, what's the news on Bert whatsit...the milkman?"

"Bert Ferring, sir. He'll live!" came the dry retort.

Richard laughed. "I gather the baby arrived safely. So when can I see him?"

"If you went along to the hospital, you'd find him there. And from what matron told me, they'll be pleased to get him out of the way for a bit. They think he's taken root. Even slept in the waiting room, I believe."

"Right. Suits me very well. I'll have a driver for this trip, please." And so he went off to the interview which gave him the first shock in the Clayton case.

His arrival at the hospital was timed perfectly; Bert was on the point of leaving with great reluctance on his part and even greater relief from all the hospital staff. Richard introduced himself and offered his driver's services to take the milkman home, which was received thankfully.

"Congratulations, Mr. Ferring, on your new baby. Boy or girl?"

"Boy, sir, and please call me Bert. Everybody else does."

On the way, Bert bubbled over about his marvelous son. Richard listened patiently and made the right noises, although, as Bert had been present at the actual birth, some of the obstetrical details nearly brought his breakfast up!

But Bert, despite his state of euphoria, apparently, was no fool. When they reached his home, he sobered down. "You'd better come in, sir. I expect you want me to talk about Mrs. Clayton. Poor lady. She was such a nice person, just about my favourite customer, I think."

The Laura Clayton Fan Club was growing by the

hour, and Richard had a strong feeling it was all genuine, not just people's disinclination to speak ill of the dead. He was beginning to wish he'd known the lady himself, but, no doubt, he'd find out a lot more about her before he was finished.

Oh, God! He suddenly remembered. *And I'll have to meet the son later on.* He wasn't looking forward to that one tiny bit.

The atmosphere of love and care hit Richard like a tangible thing as soon as he entered Bert's house. The hall and sitting room were bowers of greenery.

"The wife loves her plants," was Bert's unnecessary comment, and a sweet smell of lavender furniture polish hung in the air. A happy house, and now he had to bring one of life's worst horrors in to disturb it.

"We've got rather a tricky situation here," Richard began. "As the finder of the body you should have been carted off to the station for a full statement, but with your wife choosing the same moment to go into her act, it wasn't done. All we've got are the bare bones, so if you don't mind, we'll go through it properly now. I'm sure you want this bastard caught as much as all Mrs. Clayton's friends. So begin at the beginning and tell me all you can."

That was when Bert dropped his bombshell."Well, at least you know who did it!"

Richard stared at him. "Do we? Then I wish you'd tell me. I don't know!"

Bert gaped at Richard and then his face went crimson with agonizing embarrassment. "Oh, Jesus!" he whispered. "I didn't tell them! Oh, my God, sir, I was so taken up with Pat- the wife-it all went out of my head. I was near out of my mind with worry, and the police were kind. They let me go in the ambulance with Pat, and I never told them what Mrs. Clayton said."

Richard was flabbergasted. "What she said! Do you mean to tell me she wasn't dead when you came across her? For God's sake, man, let's have the story! Never mind about the beginnings. What happened?"

"Well you know we were on the way home from my mum's. Because of the fog, she'd lent me a torch. I was shining this on the path so that Pat wouldn't take a tumble. She was awkward, you know, sir, and I saw this body lying there. I ran up to it and bent down with Pat right beside me. I shone the torch on her face and recognized Mrs. Clayton. Then we saw the blood. Her eyes were open, but I could see she was pretty far gone. I've done first aid."

"Yes, yes, go on!" said Richard in an agony of impatience.

"I didn't touch her, because I knew it was going to be a police case, but I spoke to her. I said, 'What happened, Mrs. Clayton. Who did this', and she said two words faintly but clear enough. 'Leslie Pettitt,' she said. Then I think she died, and Pat started screaming and—"

Richard was on his feet. "Leslie Pettitt? You're quite sure, Bert? Quite sure that was the name?"

"Absolutely, sir, I'd swear to it. Do you think I'll ever forget last night?"

"May I use your phone?" Richard didn't wait for permission. He was through to the station quickly, identified himself, and gave his orders.

"I've got a name for you in connection with the Clayton murder. Leslie Pettitt. What? No, I don't know how you spell it or how many T's it's got. Get onto this right away. Telephone directories, electoral roll, anything, and everything. Ask everyone she knew if the name's familiar. Get busy! I'll be in later."

Poor Bert was sitting, looking crestfallen. "I'm so sorry, sir. I should have told somebody last night but I was..."

Richard seethed with anger but was fair-minded enough to realize that Bert, too, had his priorities, and who could really blame him for putting his wife first?

"Well, we've got it now," he said, trying to speak kindly. "Not much time lost and this information is the best lead we've had so far. Now I expect you want to wash and shave and so on, but if you'll come down to the station as soon as possible, I'd be grateful. Make a full statement and sign it. We'll take it from here."

Back at the station he was greeted with the glum information that there were dozens of Pettitt or Petitts in the phone book alone. The officers made a start on the purely local ones of whom there were about ten and only one L. Pettitt at that.

"Someone amongst her friends may know the name; I'll ring Sir John Bury first since he's known her for ages. I'll go to her home if I have no luck with him. I've got to be there anyway to meet the son. Does anyone know what time he's arriving?"

Nobody did. Richard got through to the Chief Constable without any delay. *The old boy will probably be glued to his phone from now on. Still, better that than under our feet here!*

"Sir," he began without any greeting. "Does the name Leslie Pettitt mean anything to you?"

"Pettitt? Pettitt?" Sir John mused. "Can't say it rings any bells. Why?"

Richard gave him a full account of Bert's story. Sir John was furious and began to rant.

What was the name of the misbegotten son of a peacock who'd let him go swanning off to the hospital without getting this information at the time? He'd have his guts for garters, and so on, and so on.

Richard let him rage for a bit and then changed the subject by telling him what steps were being taken to repair the damage. "And you're quite sure you've never heard the name before?"

"Can't say I have, and I knew most of the people she knew. Two of your best bets will be Milly Patcham and young Alec. They were closer to her. And by the way, you'll get them both together at Laura's house. I phoned Alec early this morning. He's shattered, of course, but said he'd leave at once. Shouldn't have usurped your authority, Hayward, but I know you'll understand."

Richard's grin was a trifle sour after he rang off. "No, you certainly shouldn't have 'usurped my authority', you old nuisance," he muttered.

This famous Mrs. Clayton was upsetting far more things and people in her death than ever she'd done in her life.

Chapter Four

"Is Milly Patchman here?" Richard asked the policeman who let him into Laura's house.

The man grimaced, jerked his head towards what was presumably the kitchen, and whispered, "She's taking this awfully hard, sir. Never known Milly when she wasn't talking."

Richard nodded, went to the open door, and looked into the sun-filled kitchen. He saw a woman in her sixties who could have posed for a painting of Grief. She was just sitting with her hands clasped together on the table in front of her. The puffy cheeks and red eyes told their own story. Richard walked up, put his hand on her shoulder gently, and said, "I'm sorry, Mrs. Patchman."

Her eyes filled with tears, her head went down on her arms, and she sobbed. Richard waited silently for the worst to blow over.

She wiped her eyes and nose on a tissue from a half empty box beside her. Voice thickened by too much crying, she said, "I can't believe it! I just can't believe it—madam dear 'gorn.' Are you a copper, too?" He nodded, and her sorrow became anger. "Then wotcher doin' about it? You find the bugger wot done it an' I'll kill 'im, Gwad 'elp me I'll do for 'im like 'e done for my dear lady."

This was a good sign. Richard explained who he was and then had the inspiration of asking if she'd like to make tea for them both and the constable in the hall. She was happier at having something to do, and while she was boiling a kettle, warming the pot, measuring out the tea, he led her on to talk about the last time she'd seen her 'madam dear'.

If he'd known her better, he'd have been surprised at the way she kept to the point, giving an almost verbatim report of what each had said and what had been done. The tears threatened again when she talked about Laura's pleasure at the prospect of a visit from Alex, and Richard's ears pricked up when she said, "and 'specially because she 'ad a problem she wanted to discuss with 'im. Now we'll never know what it was." He questioned her minutely about that, but she had no idea at all what this problem was.

"No, I 'aven't, and she never said, although I did hint that I wanted to know more. She talked about most things to me. We was close to each other, sir, but she shut up real sharp an' changed the subjick. An' if you're goin' to ask me to 'ave a guess, it's no use. I should 'ave said she was a lady as 'ad no worries at all."

She told him about the two letters that were still on the kitchen mantle shelf. Richard read them. The first was self explanatory since it was from Alec, but the second provided him with further food for thought. The envelope bore a South African stamp, but the letter itself had no address or date. It read:

My Dear Laura,

Perhaps for a surprise. I'm coming home...for good. I've not been happy since my poor old Clive died, so I've sold up, and it's back to England for me. I shall be arriving almost as soon as this letter—could be before if all we hear about your Postal service is true!

Anyway, my plane gets into Heathrow about 11:00 a.m. on Monday, April 2. I'll make straight for the Cumberland and phone you from there. Hopefully, you'll invite me down to stay for a bit while we decide where I'm going to live. I rather fancy your part of the world. Any properties going?

No news now. We'll talk the sun up when we meet. Looking forward to seeing you.

Love,

Ros.

P.S. (*Women!* thought Richard. *Never known one yet who didn't add a postscript to a letter...*) But this one caused him to think.

P.S. What an extraordinary thing about L.P. We'll certainly have to decide what to do about that!

"Mrs. Patchman. Have you any idea who wrote this letter to Mrs. Clayton? It's from South Africa and signed 'Ros'."

"Oh, that'll be Mrs. Rosemary Marden. She was at school with my lady, I believe. Got married and went to South Africa after the war, so I 'eard. I met 'er once when she come to stay on 'oliday with 'er 'usband, and my madam dear went there for a month. Oh, years ago it were, but they always write regular. The 'usband died about a year ago."

"Another question for you, and I want you to think about it extremely carefully. Have you ever heard of or heard Mrs. Clayton mention anyone called Pettitt-Leslie Pettitt?"

Milly screwed up her eyes in concentration. "Can't say as I 'ave." She thought some more and shook her head definitively. "No, never 'eard it, and I know nearly everyone. I'd've remembered if madam dear ever said it, too. I knew all 'er friends."

Richard gave no information away but contented himself by saying, "think about it, will you, please? Let me know if anything occurs to you."

Putting Ros's letter in his pocket, he thanked Milly for the tea, which, as he'd guessed, was almost too strong to drink, and told her he was leaving but would be back later to see Alec. This started her crying again.

"Now, Milly, if you'll allow me to call you that, you must try and bear up. I know it's easy for me to say, but just try and think how Laura's son's going to feel when he walks into the house. You'll have to try and comfort him, you know. Nobody else can."

The constable, still sitting in the hall, had a surprised look on his face when Richard said he was leaving. "I thought you were going to stay until Mr. Clayton gets here, sir."

"I was, but I've changed my mind. It's not fair to pounce on the poor chap the minute he arrives. He's going to have his hands full with Milly. Give him a couple of hours and then phone me. I'll come back when he's recovered a bit."

Upon his return to the station, Richard found the Pettitt enquiry in full swing, but so far, nothing promising had shown up. He read Ros's letter again and took up the phone. Half an hour later, he rang Sir John Bury again.

"Another question, sir. Have you heard of Mrs. Rosemary Marden?"

"Oh, yes," the Chief Constable answered eagerly. "Now, her I do know about. Why? What's turned up now?"

Richard told him in detail of his talk with Milly and read out the letter. Sir John jumped to the same conclusion at once. "L.P., eh? This Leslie Pettitt, do you suppose? Well, it's obvious she'd told Ros about him.

What are you doing about it?"

"I've already done it, sir. I rang a mate of mine at Scotland Yard and asked him to find out what planes are due at Heathrow from South Africa around 11:00 a.m. tomorrow morning and if Mrs. Marden is on the passenger list. If she is, he is to have her met. He'll break the news to her—poor devil, I don't envy him—and see if he can persuade her to come on down here straight away. The sooner we can talk to her, the better."

"Good work, my boy. Yes, that should clear up the Pettitt mystery. Any luck yet in tracing him from your end?"

"None so far, but we'll keep on trying. However, I have high hopes this Mrs. Marden will be able to help us. We'll keep our fingers crossed."

"I knew I could rely on you, Hayward. You've made good progress in short space of time. Keep it up!"

He hung up. Richard groaned. "That's enough to put a curse on it." He was more right than he knew; this case was only just beginning!

For the next fifteen minutes or so, he shut himself into his office for a serious rethink. His original dismissal of Laura's murder as a senseless killing was well and truly down the drain.

There seemed no doubt this Pettitt character existed. But what possible association could he have had with a woman like Laura who led him to murder? And why was it that none of those closest to her—Sir John, Milly, the vicar, and his wife who'd been talked to that morning, various members of the W.I., and other organizations—had ever heard the name? And why was it that a person living thousands of miles away had?

He recalled Milly's words once again. What problem

did 'madam dear' have to discuss with her son. Was it reasonable to assume there was a connection? Surely if she'd confided in her old friend in South Africa, she would have sought advice nearer to home. Nothing made any sense.

He just hoped to God this Rosemary Marden could do a spot of clarifying. It was possible Alec knew about it already. His mother might have written. He checked his watch impatiently. Has he given the fellow time enough to get over the trauma of entering her house?

At that precise moment, his phone rang.

"Detective Chief Inspector Hayward?"

"Speaking."

"I'm Alec Clayton. I believe you want to see me."

Richard was nonplussed momentarily. What the hell did you say in circumstances like these? Better keep it formal. "Indeed I do, Mr. Clayton, but I didn't want to rush you. I realize how difficult this must be for you."

"Difficult!" The tone was bitter. "That's an understatement if ever I heard one!"

"I'm afraid I'm not picking my words very well, but words aren't much use on occasions like this."

"You'd know better than I about such things. It's not everyday one's mother gets murdered." The voice was more acid still, but Richard recognized the raw emotion behind it.

"Sorry," the disembodied voice continued. "I needn't have said that. Would you come round here now, please? I want to get it over."

"I'm leaving right away," said Richard, hanging up the phone.

* * * *

Arriving at the Clayton house for the second time

that day, Richard stole a moment to look at the beautiful world around him. Brilliant sunshine, blue sky, green grass, birds shrieking their heads off, the sound of children shouting happily on the swings at the other side of the park—a lovely spring day. But inside the house behind him...he sighed. Ah well, get on with the thankless job.

The constable on duty was at the door before he knocked. "I'm glad to see you back, sir," he half whispered. "The poor gentleman's in a bad way. But Milly's gone, thank goodness."

As Richard stepped into the hall, the sitting room door was open, and along the floor rushed something like a furry rat, flung itself at him, smartly nipped his ankle, and then stood back, yapping in a shrill little voice. Richard scooped up a Yorkshire terrier pup with its topknot tied up in a ridiculous scarlet ribbon bow.

"So that's what you think of the fuzz, is it?" he asked the tiny creature. *Thank the Lord. This was as good an icebreaker as any.*

The man who came forward took the Yorkie from Richard and placed it on the ground when it promptly started to do battle with a corner of the fur rug in front of the fire. Both men then moved into the sitting room.

"I'm Alec Clayton, of course. You must be Chief Inspector Hayward."

Richard saw a man of about his own age, a couple of inches shorter and broader. The pleasant face was drawn, making him appear older. "Your dog?" asked Richard, to put the chap at ease before the serious business began. *Wrong question!*

"No. I had it delivered here today as a present for my mother. She is...was...a great dog lover. Her old one died a few months ago, and she wrote to tell me she was thinking of getting another. This was to be a surprise." He gave a strangled laugh. "Nothing like the surprise she's given me, is it?"

The bitterness was apparent, but he made an effort and went on talking almost compulsorily. "God knows what I'll do with the animal now. Take it back to the breeder, I suppose. We've got cats at home, also a baby." He broke off. "Oh my God! Why are we talking about cats and dogs? Sit down, please. My manners have gone to pot. I don't know what I'm doing or saying."

"Understandable," Richard said and sat, although, Alec prowled about the room. "I'm not going to put my foot in it again by saying the wrong words, so I'll keep my sympathy to myself. But we do have to talk. Now, Mr. Clayton, what can I tell you first? How much do you know of what happened?"

"Damn all!" Alec broke out. "Sir John phoned but gave no details beyond the bare facts. I'm afraid I didn't give him much chance. Hung up and raced for the car. Milly, you've met Milly, I gather, was practically incoherent, and so I got rid of her as soon as I decently could. All your chap outside would say is that you'd tell me all when you got here. So you see I'm just about going mad!"

Richard told him about the finding of the body, said she'd died almost instantaneously, for the moment added nothing on the Pettitt angle. That could come later when the poor bloke had digested this lot. When he finished, it seemed as if the truth was really getting to Alec, almost as if he'd not quite believed it before. Richard's terse, factual account made it true.

"Damn and blast him to hell, whoever he is!" Alec's

words were quiet, but the intensity of the curse was savage. He walked up and down the room, picking things up, putting them down aimlessly. His restless hands moved to a silver framed photo of his mother, and that finished him.

"She was a good old mum to me!" His voice cracked. Swiftly he did an about face and stumbled blindly to the window, keeping his back to Richard.

Richard thought no worse of him for the display of emotion. He just sat quietly and said nothing. Then he saw an unopened bottle of scotch with glasses on a tray. He stood up, opened the bottle, poured a stiff tot, and silently handed it to Alec where he stood by the window.

Alec drained the glass almost in one gulp, braced himself, and faced into the room. His mouth opened to say something, but Richard was there first.

"And if you apologize again, I'll bloody well thump you! I've got a 'good old mum' of my own, you know. If I were in your shoes, I'd be howling my blasted eyes out, and I'm used to this sort of thing as you so truly said."

Such forthright speaking from a stranger he'd met barely half an hour ago worked a minor miracle. Alec managed a small laugh. "Thanks. I needed that—both the earful and the drink. I'm going to have another. Will you join me?"

"Only a small one and the same for you. We've still got a lot to discuss, and I don't want you bombed out of your skull. Have you eaten by the way?"

"Not since dinner last night," Alec said. "Milly insisted on making me some sandwiches, but I don't fancy facing up to food yet."

Richard realized with surprise it was past lunch time, and he'd not eaten, either. "Well, I do. Wheel them in, and I'll share them with you. I'll just tell my constable what to do."

The sandwiches were appetizing, and Richard was glad to see that Alec ate a good proportion of them. Coffee was percolating, and when the dirty plates were cleared away, they sat down to the drinking of it.

Much to the police driver's disgust, he'd been dispatched to get a tin of puppy food for the Yorkie and feed it in the kitchen. Only then was he told to go and find himself something nourishing and report back in an hour.

"Not exactly what I joined the Force for!" he grumbled to the constable going off duty.

"Now!" Richard began. "I'm afraid there's quite a bit more to this sorry affair than I've told you yet, so you'd better listen carefully and see if you can help."

Alec listened quietly while Richard told him everything. A spasm of pain shot over his face when he heard that his mother hadn't died quite so quickly as he'd been led to believe, but he didn't speak. The end of the story seemed to leave him completely bewildered.

"But who the devil's Leslie Pettitt?"

"I was hoping you could tell me. Haven't you ever heard of him, either?"

"I'm damn sure I haven't. Of course, I've been away from Burshill for two years, but if he was anyone important to my mother, I'm sure she'd have mentioned him. She wrote once a week, as regular as clockwork, giving us all the local news and everything she was up to. She knew I was a bit bothered about her living here alone, so she took good care to let me know she was busy and happy."

"This problem Milly mentioned—have you any idea

what that could have been about? I wondered if it could have been simply to do with her wish to get another dog. Milly told me you weren't too keen on the idea, but that Mrs. Clayton felt she could talk you round."

Alec seemed to be considering this but shook his head. "No, there would have been no problem there. I knew, and mother knew I knew she'd be buying another dog. It's true I was against it because she was always so broken up when they died, but on the other hand, I'd have felt she was safer with one in the house."

"Even a scrap like that?" Richard smiled, indicating the Yorkie, now replete and snoring beside them.

"Oh, they're game little beggars. Well, he tackled you, didn't he?"

It pleased Richard to hear this touch of humour, but he returned to the more important topic. "We seem to have reached an impasse then. Nobody here has heard the name of this Pettitt, either, and we shall never know if it was he your mother was going to consult you about. Do you find it strange—forgive me for asking—that she should confide in Mrs. Marden instead of you?"

Richard knew Alec was observing the point he had just made by the studious look on the man's face.

"I can only think of one reason, and I don't like it! Whatever it was, I wasn't told because she knew it would worry me. I can't help wishing it is what she wanted to talk to me about. Something else strikes me. You've probably thought this out for yourself, but here goes. Aunt Ros was mother's oldest and dearest friend. They told each other everything. But, to my knowledge, they'd only actually met about three times at most since the war which was a helluva long time ago. Now, if Aunt Ros is the only person who knew this Pettitt, mustn't it have been to do with something which happened donkeys' years ago before she moved to South Africa?"

This was, indeed, one of the vague thoughts which had passed through Richard's mind earlier. It made sense, but...

"Your mother also had many old and dear friends closer to home. What about Sir John Bury, for instance? If there was anything nasty cropping up, who better than a Chief Constable to go to?"

They kicked the subject around for quite a while but got no further. Richard began to think the interview had produced all that was relevant. He rose to leave.

"Perhaps we'll get some answers when Mrs. Marden arrives," he said. "How long do you mean to stay? I expect she'd like to see you."

"Oh, I'll be here for quite a while. My wife and baby are coming down tomorrow, and I've been given an extended leave of absence until everything's cleared up."

"That's good. They'll be a great comfort to you. I'll keep in close touch."

"I'd like that, and thanks for being such a super copper, if I may say so."

Richard felt uncomfortable. He'd done little enough so far. Suddenly, he was struck with another thought. "Look here, Clayton. About the little dog. Are you really going to send him back to the breeder?"

"I shall have to. Pity. He's a nice little chap."

"Then let me buy him off you." Richard was surprised to hear himself saying these words. "I'd like to give him to my mother. She's a dog lover, too. He'd have a good home."

There was no need for him to add that the dreadful business had made him appreciate his own mother more.

It would have sounded too sickly sentimental and wasn't his normal style at all. But Alec knew. What's more he absolutely, categorically refused to accept Richard's cheque, hard as he protested.

"I can't do that. Regulations forbid me accepting presents."

"I'm not giving you anything. In any other circumstance it'd sound nauseating, but today I can be allowed to say anything I choose. The dog is a present from my mother to yours."

There was no answer to that! Richard walked out of the house, carrying the Yorkie.

The driver took one look at the dog, and said brightly, "a suspect, sir, being taken in for questioning?"

Richard scowled so forbiddingly, the man looked as though he was about to jump out of his shoes. "You can take me direct to my home, constable, and wait for me. I'm leaving the dog there."

The puppy food was brought up, quite messily, on the floor of the car. It relieved Richard's feelings considerably to say to the driver when they arrived at the house, "and clear that lot up before I come out again!"

Chapter Five

Ella, after the initial shock of having this new member of the family thrust on her, was delighted. She fell in love with the small thing at once, and the feeling was mutual.

"Oh, Richard, you couldn't have given me a nicer present."

"It's not from me," he said brusquely, giving her a brief run-down on the circumstances. Her kind heart was touched.

"Poor young man," she said with real sympathy. "I wish I could do something to help. Do you think I could phone and thank him?"

"Don't see why not, but I'd leave it for a day or so. He's still shot to pieces over this ghastly business. I'll tell you the details when I get back this evening. Shouldn't think I'll be too late. There isn't a lot I can do until the morning."

Ella knew her son well. He didn't have to spell out the details of how she'd come to be the owner of this gorgeous little ball of fun.

Richard added sternly as he was leaving again, "And I don't want his visiting cards all over my new carpets, so see to it, Mother."

The wretched driver, red-faced and sweating, had made a fair job of the cleaning but ostentatiously left all the windows wide open on the way back to the Station. Richard could imagine the comments there would be from that quarter when the fellow joined his mates!

* * * *

Good progress had been made with the Pettitts in the phone book, but nothing concrete emerged.

"We found two Leslies locally, sir, but one's about ninety and nearly gaga. The other's a butcher, and he was at an all-night party in the bosom of his family. Afraid we're coming to the end of them, at least any of them who live in the county."

With the idea in mind that the Pettitt he was after might not be a local at all, Richard wasn't too disappointed. All his hopes were pinned now on Rosemary Marden, winging her way home from South Africa. He focused his attention on the mountainous pile of paper work on the desk. Hadn't anybody done anything while he was laid up, for God's sake?

To the tap on his door, he shouted "Come in!"

One of the younger detective-sergeants stood before him, looking ill at ease. His shout must have sounded more belligerent than he felt. Richard had already marked this particular man down as promising material. Ordinary in appearance unless you looked closely at the keen eyes, the sergeant had the ability to melt into the surroundings at will—a valuable attribute which Richard could never achieve because of his six foot two frame. Now what was his name?

"Findon, isn't it? Well, what can I do for you?"

Richard could tell that Jim Findon wasn't exactly scared of his new Detective Chief Inspector. All the officers were treading warily. Not a surprise considering Richard had heard one of his colleagues remark, "He reminds me of the quotation about somebody or other, that he was a beast but a just beast. Reckon our new DCI is one of that kind."

Findon was firm in his resolve to speak his thoughts. "I've had an idea, sir, about the Clayton murder."

"Have you now? Well, I don't mind telling you any contributions will be most gratefully accepted. Fire away."

"Well, has it occurred to you that this Leslie Pettitt might be a female?"

It hadn't. Richard was startled. "Good God, Sergeant. You could be right, and no, it hadn't occurred to me. But Leslie's a girl's name as well as a boy's, of course. The spelling would be different, of course, 'Ley' instead of 'Lie.' Now that is, indeed, a thought. Hang about while I phone our doctor."

His question to the doctor was brief. "Could Mrs. Clayton's stab wound have been inflicted by a woman?"

Doctors, especially police doctors, always hesitate to commit themselves. This one was no exception. He hemmed and hawed but finally agreed, rather doubtfully, that it was just about possible. "It wouldn't have taken brute strength. A certain amount of force would be needed, but if it was done in anger, she might have had the incentive."

"I hardly imagine a murder committed without anger!" was Richard's dry rejoinder. "Thanks, doc. That's all I wanted to know."

Replacing the receiver, he eyed Findon thoughtfully. "Well done, Sergeant. No medical reason why a woman couldn't have done it. I do think our Doctor Leigh's old-fashioned. He didn't seem convinced that a woman could commit the crime."

Jim Findon laughed, obviously well pleased with the reception of his brainwave.

"But I don't know where it gets us," Richard

continued, damping the Sergeant's enthusiasm a trifle. "We'll have to wait and see. But if you get any more bright ideas, bring them to me, however daft they may sound. I've had plenty of my own daft notions, and sometimes, only sometimes, mind you, they've paid off."

With his smiling dismissal of Findon, Richard was well aware he'd made an ally and a good one at that. The others would follow in time he was sure.

He let himself off the chain reasonably early and drove home. An early night wouldn't come amiss after his few hours sleep of the morning. He'd forgotten all about the new addition and was reminded of it forcibly when he opened his door. A few inches of yapping fury barred his way, willing to die for his new mistress. Richard burst into a hearty laugh at the ridiculous sight; his mother bustled forward to retrieve her new champion.

"Now, Fuzz! Behave yourself. This is a friend."

"What did you call him?" An incredulous Richard thundered.

"Fuzz—that's what I've decided shall be his name. You told me what you said at your first meeting, and I think it suits him."

"Charming!" Richard then took in the rest of the room and laughed helplessly. "When I proposed to Kate, I promised her she should have a mixture of the Taj Mahal, Buckingham Palace, and the Garden of Eden. Look what she's got! Well, at least we've got the fertilizer for the garden!"

Every inch of floor was covered in thick wedges of newspaper, ominously sprinkled here and there, with one larger offering smack in front of the fireplace. Other areas were occupied by a dog basket, a bowl of water, another of food, and a rubber bone.

"I wonder how she'll take to living in a kennel instead."

Ella drew herself up to her full five foot three inches in height. "Now you're being silly. We're getting really organized. He's extremely good. That little woopsie was done in the excitement of hearing you coming!"

"A likely story!"

"The bowls and basket will live in the kitchen, and already he knows what the garden is for. Anyway, we shall go when Kate comes home, so you'll have your beautiful house to yourselves. Go and look round upstairs, and you'll see how busy we've been today."

"Very impressive," was his comment after the tour of inspection. "You're an angel, Mother, and I won't say another unkind word."

"That'll be the day!" Ella scoffed.

When they'd eaten, he made a beeline for his stock of records. Music was as necessary to this unorthodox copper as breathing. He'd met his darling Kate at a concert, and now, it was doubly precious.

The few people who knew him well were aware that his choice of music at any given time reflected his mood. His mother was one of those people. "A little Bach?" she enquired innocently, glancing at Fuzz. Richard threw a cushion at her and settled down to some Delius. Evidently, he had a quiet mind tonight.

The quiet was shattered at bedtime. Fuzz was tucked up comfortably in his basket in the kitchen when the two humans went upstairs. The dog obviously wasn't pleased at this arrangement, and his shrill, heart-rendering whining at the foot of the stairs was more than Ella could bear. Fuzz and his basket were carried up to her bedroom, where he snored gently for the rest of the night.

"Most unhygienic," Richard grumbled the next morning but was so amazed when the little creature trotted out into the garden and did his duty there that all was forgiven. Ella rated the achievement as roughly the equivalent of the first moon landing. No doubt at all the gift of the dog was an unqualified success. He left for the station with a broad grin on his face.

* * * *

The hours dragged as he waited for the all-important call from London. His friend at Scotland Yard had promised to go personally to Heathrow and ring Richard as soon as he'd made contact.

Eleven o'clock. She should be landing. Allow half an hour for customs clearance and baggage collection.

Midday passed. One o'clock came. He wouldn't leave his office, so he sent out for coffee and a sandwich. At one fifteen, the phone rang. He pounced on it; yes, it was the Scotland Yard man.

"Richard? Bad news. We've lost her."

"What the devil do you mean you lost her? All right, so you know where she went—the Cumberland. Get her there, man."

"You don't understand. When I say, we've lost her, that's it. Finito. She's dead."

"What!" Richard shouted and stood up, breathless with shock. "How? What happened, for God's sake?"

"She was murdered, stabbed like your woman. At Heathrow."

Richard stumbled back a little, but he managed to collect himself. "Tell me about it in detail."

"Well, for a kick-off, I was a bit late arriving due to a traffic snarl-up, and unfortunately, her plane arrived early

56

about the first time in history, I should say. When I got there, I made straight for the Arrivals terminal. I was hit by a crowd of passengers, police, airport officials, God knows who. The ambulance men were just taking her away. I've been making enquiries ever since. It'll be our pigeon, of course, but I think you'd better come up, Richard. We've got to talk."

* * * *

"Nobody saw a bloody thing! The same old story." Detective Chief Inspector Geoffrey Brede was bitter. "Everybody milling about, waiting for their luggage to come off the conveyor belt, grabbing it, and not looking at anything else. That plane was just about full to capacity, and there were a hell of a lot of passengers."

"And?" Richard prompted.

"Suddenly, your Mrs. Marden slumped right onto the belt as it was moving. At first, people thought she'd fainted, and it was quite a while before the thing was stopped. By then, of course, she'd fallen off it. Some woman saw her, and the blood and began to scream. You can imagine the pandemonium after that."

"In which the murderer got clear away!" Richard slammed his fist down on the desk, cursing vehemently.

Before catching the London train, he'd rung Sir John, and the Chief Constable's reactions were predictable—disbelief, shock, anger, in that order. "Who the hell knew where and when she was landing?" Sir John asked, though he quickly responded with what he already knew. "Oh God! I expect all Burshill knows!"

Richard echoed the groan. "Oh, no! Not Milly Patcham?"

"Afraid so. I called on young Clayton yesterday soon after you left. Milly was back. Can't keep away I suppose, poor old dear. She was busy doing out the guest room. Alec wanted to invite Ros to stay if you managed to get her down here. Milly knew about it, so that could be the answer."

Richard hadn't time to delve into the puzzle at that particular point. He'd barely make the fast train as it was. Promising to phone again when he could, he was away.

Now he was closeted with his old friend, Geoffrey Brede. After a few hours of intensive work, Rosemary Marden's luggage, handbag, and pockets had been inspected; nothing helpful was there.

Richard's forlorn hope that Laura's last letter might have been amongst her things was dashed. Even Mrs. Marden's address book had no English entries except for Laura's. She didn't appear to have kept a diary. Any clues to the murder were nil.

"We'll have to wait until her heavy stuff arrives to look through it. I understand it's coming by sea. We've contacted some of the people in the address book; all were horrified and mystified. No family, so we'll get no answers there. Sorry to sound pessimistic, but it looks as if the secret, whatever it was, has died with her."

Brede had been given a full account of the Clayton murder, and both men agreed that the coincidence was too great to ignore.

"Somebody's being very clever—ice-cold reflexes, nerves of steel, and split second timing. Use all the clichés you can remember; this chap's got 'em all. But what in God's name could two elderly women have known to drive him to these extremes? I've never known a case like it, and I'm damned if I know where we're gong to start. Looks as if I'm passing the buck, but I think our villain must come from your patch. We'll have to work together on this one."

"And I've got a Chief Constable breathing down my neck!" Richard said. "Seems he was once smitten with the lady about a hundred years ago, and he's stuck his ear with glue to the phone, waiting for me to crack the case with my usual panache."

"Serves you right for being the boy wonder!" Geoff laughed at him. "Where are you going to start now that your only lead's died on you?"

"God knows! Normally, I'd begin by digging into the lady's past, but her past's just as much of an open book as her last years. Lived in the same house forty years, everybody knew and liked her, including police and clergy. Not to mention that fearsome daily, Milly Patcham. I shouldn't think her 'madam dear' blew her nose without Milly knowing and broadcasting it."

"You'll probably finish up arresting your CC in sheer desperation. Unrequited love or something and it has taken rather a long while to sink in that she wouldn't have him!"

"Silly clot!" Richard was amused at the suggestion all the same. "Trouble with that theory is the old boy told me himself they'd both made happy marriages and stayed good friends. Somebody wasn't a good friend to her, that's for sure!"

Around teatime, he made his way back to Burshill. Seeing the crowd of commuters traveling on the same train, he made a mental note to send Sergeant Findon along when the rush died down to ask if any Burshill residents, other than the business fraternity, had made trips to London that morning. The station staff was a friendly lot and knew most of the town's older population.

But, of course, the murderer would have been far more likely to go by car to avoid recognition. Richard thought of his use of the phrase 'older generation'; all the bits and pieces coming together in his mind were forcing him to the conclusion that the roots were in the past. Therefore, this killer must be someone around the Laura/Rosemary age group.

Ah! But suppose it's a son or even grandson starting up an old vendetta again? Richard frowned. Oh, for God's sake, shut up, you silly so-and-so.

Sergeant Findon took his instructions about the railway station but the look on his face told Richard he didn't have much hope that he would gain any more information. After listening to Richard's story of the London day, he silently handed him a copy of the local "Evening Cryer."

There on the front page, breaking news, was an account of the Heathrow murder, linking it to the Clayton killing by virtue of the friendship between the two women. To his disgust, there was a reference to himself, stating, quite erroneously, that he would be in charge of both crimes.

"That'll please Scotland Yard!" he said with a grin. "But the Cryer got hold of this very quickly. Smart bit of work on someone's part."

Sergeant Findon cleared his throat and said. "As a matter of fact, sir, Milly Patcham lives next door to one of the Cryer's reporters. She heard the news on the radio about the Heathrow job and was round to his back door like a shot!"

Richard had heard just about enough of Milly for one day. "I think I'll run her in for the murder, Sergeant. It'll get her out of our hair for a bit. Now I'll phone the CC and then I'm going home."

That evening after dinner, Wagner's Ride of the Valkries went on the turntable at full throttle. The music was so loud that Ella and Fuzz decided to have another early night.

Most of Tuesday, Richard seemed to spend on the phone. Geoff Brede had been busy, more calls to the people in Rosemary's address book, and a long talk to her local police chief. All abortive. As luck would have it, the plane she'd taken had been filled with mostly conference representatives. Even though they were questioned in depth, no one seemed to know or had seen anything.

None of them had known her previously. No one could even remember standing by her as the luggage was coming in. The crowd was constantly shifting as they made a snatch at their own bags. In fact, as Geoff summed it up succinctly when he said to Richard, "I'm as hoarse as a crow and spitting feathers with bugger-all to show for it."

Richard took half an hour away from his office after lunch to call on Alec Clayton. He'd no doubt the news had reached the Clayton house, but he felt he should report in person.

The door was opened this time by a young woman dressed in a black sweater and skirt who introduced herself as Jane Clayton. She showed him into the sitting-room where, to his utter surprise, he found his mother. She was sitting with a baby in her arms, looking quite at home. Fuzz was knocking the hell out of his rubber bone on a sheet of the Times.

"What the...?" he began.

"Hullo, dear," Ella said brightly. "These nice young people asked me to come round, so here I am."

Alec came forward; he appeared to be much better today, Richard was thankful to note.

"I rang your mother this morning since I remembered I hadn't told you about the dog's injections. Mrs. Hayward was so sweet, so I asked her to pop in and meet my wife and son. We only need your wife to complete the family gathering."

Richard's face clouded over, and Alec quickly changed the subject. "I suppose you've come about Aunt Ros? Sir John phoned yesterday and told me. This is getting worse and worse, isn't it?"

Richard told his attentive audience what had happened to date, but as he'd expected, there were no useful contributions from this quarter. He spoke of the theory that it might be something from the past which had caught up to the two ladies. "Do you have any ideas about that Alec."

"I don't know an awful lot about my mother's life before I was born. She and my father had only been married a few years when I arrived, and I've never lived anywhere but here till I married. My grandparents died before I was old enough to know them very well, and Mother never talked much about her early life. I gather there was some money in the family which she, as an only child, inherited, but beyond that...well, I suppose I wasn't interested. Kids aren't, you know. They can't imagine a world they had no part in."

Ella chimed in. "That's true. There's nothing sinister about it at all. For instance, how much do you know about my early life? Go on, be honest now."

Richard admitted he knew precious little about his mother's origins. As Alec said, he'd never been particularly interested. "Fair enough." Turning again to

Alec, he asked, "Would you mind thinking about it though? Write down all you do know, however little—where your mother and father lived before marriage, mother's maiden name—that sort of thing. I'm so bogged down at the moment, who knows where we might hit pay dirt..."

* * * *

On that evening, the records had a rest while Ella aired her views on the young Claytons, of whom she approved thoroughly. Richard half listened, trying to figure out his next move.

The next move came to him in most unexpected guise. As soon as Richard entered his office, Findon brought in a letter. "I guessed you'd want to see this straight away, sir. Doesn't sound like one of our usual crackpots."

The letter was addressed to "The Officer in Charge of the Clayton Case, c/o Burshill Police Station." The address inside was from a small town about fifty miles away and ran as follows:

Dear Sir,

I was most distressed to read of the deaths of first Laura Clayton and secondly Rosemary Marden. Although we lost touch many years ago, there was a short period in our youth when the three of us were very close.

Now my reason for writing. I'm not a woman given to fanciful ideas, but the name Leslie Pettitt, mentioned in an account of the first death, rings a faint bell in my mind. The story is too long-winded to tell by letter or phone, but if you think it worthwhile, I would be glad to talk to you or any other police officer.

As I am crippled with arthritis, it is impossible for me to come to you. I go into our local Cottage Hospital tomorrow for a minor operation and expect to stay there for a week, but if you care to visit I should be pleased to see you.

However, I must warn you my theory is so ridiculous you may not even consider it. I leave it to you to judge.

Yours sincerely,

Clare Sidley

Richard drew a long breath and read the letter again. "You've read this I take it? What do you think?"

Jim Findon answered. "I think it's the real McCoy, sir. You can tell by the writing she's fairly old and, as she says, arthritic. It must have been painful to put all that down. I'd say it was genuine, but whether it means anything or not, I wouldn't like to say. She says herself it'd be ridiculous, doesn't she?"

"So's this whole bloody business. Anyway, we'll see what she has to say. First off, get the number for this local Cottage hospital she mentions. Should find it in the phone book."

When Richard got through to the hospital after Findon had found the number, he asked to speak with someone in authority. After a great deal of muffled consultation at the hospital end, he was connected to a vinegary voice which identified itself as Matron. Richard was a bit doubtful Miss Vinegar-Voice was authoritative enough for his purpose but decided it would do for a start.

"I am Detective Chief Inspector Hayward from Burshill," he announced in what sounded to his own ears a pompous tone. "I wish to make enquiries about a patient who I believe was admitted today. A Miss or Mrs. Clare Sidley."

"Miss Sidley. What's she done?" came the superior sounding voice.

"Done? Nothing at all. I'm merely asking if she is or will be coming in for an operation. This is important, and I'd be grateful for an immediate answer."

Pompous or not, his manner got a swift response. After a short interval, Matron came back.

"Miss Sidley was admitted yesterday. She had an operation on her hip this morning and is recovering quite comfortably at this moment."

Richard drew a sigh of relief and smiled. Though, with his luck running at an all-time low, she may well have died under the anesthetic!

"Good!" he said. "Now, it's necessary I come to see her. When is the earliest you can allow?"

Matron was softened by the tactful request. "Well now, best leave her for today, but she'll be quite up to receiving visitors tomorrow. I gather this is an official visit, so you needn't stick to regular hours. I hope, though, you won't be upsetting her. She's an elderly lady who's almost constantly in pain. I shall tell her you're coming, by the way."

"Perfectly in order," Richard concurred graciously. "She'll be expecting me. And which ward is she in?"

"Women's Surgical. Anyone will direct you."

Richard was about to hang up when a thought struck him. "Matron," he said hastily before she could replace the receiver. He hesitated.

"Yes?" came the impatient voice.

"This may sound a peculiar question, but what's the security like in your hospital?"

There was a pause. In an overly-loud voice, Matron said, "Security? What on earth do you mean?"

"Exactly what I say. Do you have security checks at night, for instance? Are your patients sure of their safety, know they'll be free from assault, that kind of thing?"

He dare not be more explicit but even that was enough to draw the bung right out of the vinegar barrel.

"Inspector Hayward! This is a hospital not a lunatic asylum. There are doctors and nurses about all the time. At night, a nurse is on duty in every ward. I have never had a case of robbery, assault, or murder in my hospital!"

The phone crashed down with such force it nearly sent Richard permanently deaf. "Strewth!" he blurted. "What a dragon. I don't look forward to facing her in the morning. You'd better drive me there, Findon, in case I need protection."

"I shouldn't think there was much chance of anyone nobbling Miss Sidley, though, sir. If she's in the surgical ward, there'll be plenty of old biddies ready to scream the place down if an intruder popped up."

Richard shivered. "Keep the good thoughts, Findon."

He was still massaging his ear when Sir John Bury walked in. All three officers got to their feet.

"Just passing," the Chief Constable informed them. "Any developments?"

"Yes, quite a promising one."

Richard handed the letter to him, and the Constable read it with growing excitement. "I say! This sounds like a break, Hayward. You'll go yourself, of course?"

Richard recounted the tale of the phone call and said he and Findon would be away bright and early. "Did you know Miss Sidley, sir?"

"Never heard of her, but then if she hadn't seen Mrs.

Clayton since their youthful days, it would have been before my acquaintance began. I met Laura–let's see now–it would have been 1940, I suppose. I was in the Army by then, and Laura, although I didn't know it at the time, practically engaged to Clayton." He sighed. "Things happened so fast in those days, we barely had time to think. Oh, well, let's hope we're really getting somewhere at last."

The optimism engendered by Clare Sidley's letter restored some of the ebullience he'd lost since Laura's death, and it was unfortunate he walked into the "Cryer's" crime reporter on his way out.

Seeing Sir John, the man jumped to the conclusion that things were on the move. He requested an interview. The Chief Constable declined but couldn't resist telling the reporter they were following a new lead.

"Damned old fool!" Richard grumbled to his mother that night. "Why can't he keep his trap shut? Like as not, this will turn out another dead end."

Chapter Six

Richard was fidgety and bad-tempered at breakfast next morning, and his only response to Ella's question was that he'd spent a restless night, longing to get going, to hear what this Sidley woman's 'ridiculous theory' was.

A letter from Kate, which his mother handed him, should have cheered him but didn't. Ella watched him reading it out of the corner of her eye. She could tell it was a short letter and didn't seem to contain any news he wanted.

"Everything all right with Kate?" she asked casually.

"Suppose so!" was the grudging reply. "Says she's glad we've moved in by now and sends you her love. And that's about it." His disappointment was so obvious Ella's heart ached for him. *It's not fair*, she thought. *'Specially with all this other worry on his plate.* She'd a good mind to write to Kate herself and ask what she was playing at. *But he'd kill me if I did. No, Ella, don't interfere.*

* * * *

Sergeant Findon must have sensed that Richard was jumpy, so the drive was made in almost complete silence.

The Cottage Hospital, when they reached it, proved to be a most peculiar place, not much more than a collection of Nissen huts. In fact, they were originally just that. During the war, they were occupied by the army then eventually sold off and restored as a hospital complex. But nothing drab about it; plenty of growing things around, neat grass paths between each hut, and spacious grounds in which the convalescing could walk about and enjoy the gardens.

They asked at the gate for the Woman's Surgical Ward.

"Police?" The doorman asked with more excitement than seemed warranted. "Take the third path on your left, and you'll find it signposted."

Findon looked puzzled. "How the deuce did he know we're police?"

"Probably the dragon told him to look out for us." But Richard's gut feeling was beginning to tell him something quite nasty. "Put your foot down, Sergeant."

Richard's head whipped around when he saw the ambulance and the police car. "Oh God!" Oh God!" It wasn't blasphemy as much as it was a prayer.

Richard was out of the car before it came to a standstill and was running, with his warrant card in his hand, toward the driver who was climbing into the seat of the ambulance.

"Who's in there?" he demanded, showing his card.

"A Miss Sidley, sir. She's been stabbed."

"Dead?"

"As a doornail," the man said, and with an earsplitting screech of the tires, drove off.

Richard was consumed with a blinding, savage rage, almost primeval in its intensity. Pushing everybody to one side, he strode through the door of the hut labeled Women's Surgical. He found himself in a narrow hall leading to a large open ward. He saw a small office to the left full of people in white coats.

Entering the office, Richard almost shouted, "Which of you is the Matron?"

A buxom woman, most of the starch knocked out of her, said she was. Richard eyed her up and down.

"So you've never had an assault, a robbery, or murder in your hospital, have you? There's a first time for everything, isn't there?"

"Who are you?" she enquired, drawing the remnants of dignity and sanity around her.

Richard told her who he was and then proceeded to freeze the air all round with the most scathing invective he'd ever used. Findon pulled Richard's sleeve, muttering, "Steady on, sir." Richard shook his hand off, but the flow was stemmed.

Matron, whose face had shown interesting gradations of color from brilliant scarlet to ashy white and back, recovered herself with a telling point. "If you had any reason to think this would happen, why didn't you tell me yesterday? Better still, why didn't you ask our local police to keep an eye on the poor soul?"

If she'd known how much this remark hurt Richard—what a load of guilt he was trying to shuck off by laying into her—she would have been satisfied. Maybe even sorry.

"Too late now for recriminations," he said more quietly. At that moment, to help ease the tension, a member of the local CID walked in. Richard asked Findon to clear the room, leaving only himself, the CID man, and Matron.

Richard briefly gave the CID the reason for his presence without going into details. He asked Matron to tell them what had happened. She sat down with a puckered look of dislike and began her story.

"Miss Sidley had her operation yesterday morning, and it was a success. However, during the evening, after visiting hours, she showed signs of running a temperature. To give her a bit more peace and quiet, she was moved into a private room, a single room where she would be on her own."

So much for Findon's "screaming old Biddies in the public ward", Richard thought.

"Where is this private room?" Richard asked.

"I'll show you if you'll follow me."

The private room was in the same passage as the office. There were three of them in a row, and the one allotted to Miss Sidley was that nearest the door. Richard walked into the room where everything appeared to be in order. Not even a sign of a struggle.

"Go on." The local man seemed content to let Richard do the interrogating.

"The sister on duty popped in on her from time to time during the night. The fever abated, and Miss Sidley was sleeping normally. At about six o'clock, she rang for a bedpan and was given a cup of tea."

For a moment, Matron's manner became almost human. "We all knew Miss Sidley well. She'd been a patient here off and on for years. Miss Sidley told Sister she didn't want to be disturbed for a breakfast she didn't want, Sister agreed that she need not be disturbed and could sleep on." The official voice came back. "A pity the rules were broken. We may not have been able to prevent what happened, but we might have discovered it sooner."

"When did you find out she was dead?"

"Not until about half an hour or so before you arrived. Nurse went in to wake her, realized something was wrong, and on closer inspection, thought she was dead. She called Sister, and when they turned back the sheet, they saw..." She shuddered. "It had nothing to do with her condition or operation, Miss Sidley had been stabbed to death."

"In view of what you said yesterday, do you still maintain that a stranger would be noticed?"

Matron hesitated. "Obviously I can't... At that hour of the day, although it seems an ungodly time to outsiders, there's a great deal of coming and going. As you can see for yourselves, the wards are all separate. If a man put on a white coat, we'd naturally assume he was a doctor or student on his way to another part of the grounds. We don't know everybody here, and the staff's changing constantly."

"So the only risk the killer took was when he was actually in the room. Is that it?"

"I suppose so." Matron sounded weary and dispirited.

"One more question from me, Matron, and then I'll leave this to the local men. You spoke of visiting hours. Did Miss Sidley have any visitors?"

"Of course. Her sister came."

"And the address, please." Richard's heart was thudding. Findon took out the car keys in readiness.

"She lived with Miss Sidley. I'll find the address."

"Don't bother. We've got that." Richard could hardly wait to take his leave. He flung a few brief words to the CID. "I'll call in at your Station later. Give me directions how to get to this address in the quickest possible time." He produced a copy of Clare Sidley's letter and was given a clear route then he and Findon took off.

In the car, he said, "Let's not make it four in a row, Sergeant!"

* * * *

Jim Findon knew he could break every traffic regulation in the book with his superior's blessing. Actually though, he couldn't speed through the streets -

there were too many people about so he hadn't much chance to show Richard his driving skills.

"Three poor women. Three poor devils who'd never hurt a fly, I shouldn't think," Richard muttered. "There's a jinx on this case—a bloody hoodoo—and old ladies are being put out of the way while I do bugger-all to prevent it. I'll never forgive myself if someone else dies. Never."

Findon sympathized with Richard but knew from his training it was fatal to become personally involved. He sought about for something to say to cool the situation and, he finally found some words.

"I've had another thought, sir."

"Oh? What is it this time?"

"Nothing constructive about the murders, I'm afraid, but about the three ladies themselves. We've been thinking and talking of them as 'old ladies', but they weren't old as age goes today. Mrs. Clayton's dossier tells us she'd just passed her fiftieth birthday, and if the other two women were girlhood friends of hers, they would have been about the same, wouldn't they? Not exactly senile, sir."

Richard shifted restlessly in his seat; and said to Findon, "For a fleeting second I wish I hadn't given up smoking when I got married—a cigarette would have helped calm me down." Then he added irritably, "Of course they weren't senile, but what's that got to do with anything?"

"Well, sir, I don't know how old your mother is, and I wouldn't dream of asking, but when I picked you up this morning and met her, I couldn't help thinking she'd stand up for herself. I can't imagine her sitting quietly while somebody came at her with a knife or whatever. She'd have struggled, wouldn't she? And there was no sign that any of the three put up any resistance at all."

Richard tapped one finger against his cheek. "Hold on, Sergeant. Consider the circumstances in each case. Mrs. Clayton was attacked in the park in thick fog. Mrs. Marden was killed amongst a crowd at the airport. Miss Sidley, just recovering from an operation and helpless in bed, was in no condition to fight. They were all caught on the hop."

"Yes, agreed," Findon said, "but none of them were stabbed in the back, sir. They were stabbed from the front. The victims may have been taken by surprise, but if they recognized an enemy, surely they could have screamed at least, and in each case there were people around to hear and look. Even Mrs. Clayton in the park would have been heard by the milkman and his wife, even if they couldn't have seen much. So why did none of them scream, sir?"

"An interesting point, Sergeant..." Richard frowned. "I think we can assume they knew the killer. With the first two ladies, they didn't imagine any threat to their lives. With Miss Sidley it was different. She must have had her suspicions when she wrote to me, but she was asleep when she was either struck or muffled with a pillow. In her weakened state, there would have been no time to utter."

Richard turned to face Findon abruptly. "My dear God! How many more are on the list?"

Findon breathed a sigh of relief that they'd reached their destination at this juncture. A vast difference here to the beautiful Clayton house. Miss Sidley had lived in a small villa-type residence in a street where all the houses were rather shabby and in need of repair.

"Do you want me to come in, sir?"

"Not to begin with. I'll call if I need you. Just hope to God the sister's in."

* * * *

He knocked, but there was no answer. He knocked again and then heard footsteps coming to the door. It was opened by an elderly woman, short and stocky in build. Her eyes were hard, expression severe, and clothes frumpy.

"Yes?" she asked.

Richard explained who he was and asked if he might come in. Only then did it occur to him to wonder if she knew what had happened. Surely she'd have been informed.

"I've come about your sister," he began tentatively.

"Half sister!" she corrected him tonelessly. "I've just been talking to Matron on the phone. She said you'd be calling."

Her eyes were dry, no sign of any emotion whatsoever. She ushered him into a cold, cheerless, little room. Everything was scrupulously clean but old-fashioned and battered. *No gracious living here for the poor arthritic Miss Sidley*, he thought with compassion.

"You were told what happened to your half-sister, did you say? Is your name Sidley, also, or are you married? Forgive the questions at a time like, this but there are several things I need to know urgently."

In the same toneless voice, the woman replied. "I'm Alison Sidley. We had the same father but different mothers. I'm ten years older than Clare. You needn't bother about the proprieties either, Chief Inspector. Clare and I weren't all that close. In fact, we'd practically lost touch all together, but when her arthritis got really bad, I felt it my duty to come and look after her."

God help poor Clare. This sanctimonious old bag could have been no barrel of laughs!

"Very good of you," he said, turning his head slightly and grimacing. "Now, did you know she'd written to me a few days before this dreadful occurrence?"

"I did. I told her to mind her own business and keep out of it, but oh no! She wouldn't listen and look what's come of it!"

Richard didn't dare hope, but he was determined to squeeze every last drop of information he could out of her since she was the first witness who might have something to tell him of relevance.

"This could be of the utmost importance..." he looked at her with a grave expression on his face. "Your sister is the third woman to have been murdered in almost as many days, and anything you can tell me is vital. And don't worry. I'll see you have police protection until it's cleared up."

She laughed scornfully. "I don't need your protection because I don't know anything! Your murderer would be wasting his time trying to silence me."

Richard persevered. He took Clare's letter from his wallet and gave it to the old trout. "Have you read this before?"

She adjusted her National Health spectacles and read it through. "Silly fool!" was her less than charitable comment. "Why couldn't she leave well alone!"

"What was this theory she held?"

"No idea!"

Richard's heart sank, but he had to keep trying. "Come now, Miss Sidley. You told her not to interfere so you must have known she was going to write. What was she going to tell me?"

"She didn't say, and I didn't ask," was the uncompromising reply.

He'd had enough. Time to get tough. He went to the door and called Jim Findon. When the Sergeant entered the dull room, Richard spoke.

"Sergeant Findon, I want you to take notes, if you please. Miss Sidley is being most uncooperative, and I'm treating her from now on as a person who is hindering my investigation. Get out your notebook."

Alison Sidley looked shaken. She stated that in her sixty years of life, nothing like this had ever happened to her before.

"What else do you want to know?" she asked sullenly.

"That's better," Richard said at his sternest. "For starters, you can tell me when and where your half-sister met Mrs. Clayton and Mrs. Marden. Or is that something else you don't know?"

"They were all pupils at a finishing school in France before the war." There was ineffable contempt in her voice as she said 'finishing school', and she looked around with a sneer at her present poverty-stricken surroundings. "By the time father married her mother, he'd made a bit of money, and nothing was too good for his precious Clare." The naked envy in the woman was almost tangible.

"And they kept the friendship up afterwards?"

"Not for long. I was still at home when she came back, but just after the war started, father died, and there was no more money. Clare was too proud to go on writing to people like them. She had to go out to work the same as I did. We drifted apart, and as I told you, didn't come together again till she got so bad she could hardly move about."

"So for all you know, there could have been further meetings which you didn't hear about."

"Oh, no, there weren't, Mr. Clever Policeman." She sneered at Richard. "When this murder business cropped up, I asked her why she should bother with people she hadn't seen for years. She said it was because they were such lovely girls when they were at school. Lovely girls! Anyone can be lovely when they've got money."

Findon shot a look at Richard. His expression showed what he thought of the old hag.

"All right." Richard kept his patience. "Tell me what happened about the letter. It says she read about the murders in the paper. What did she say about them?"

"Nearly had a fit to start with, but she could see I wasn't interested. Then she went off into a sort of trance. Next thing was, right out of the blue, she said to me, 'I think I know who may have done these murders.' I told her not to be a fool, but she said she'd got to let somebody know. She asked if I'd write the letter for her because her hands weren't up to it, but I've got no time for such foolishness, and in the end she did it herself."

Richard thought of that straggly handwriting and could have strangled the old witch himself! Findon looked as if he was about to do it!

"It must have been a painful effort on her part," Richard said. "Didn't it occur to you she must have felt deeply about the matter to have gone to so much trouble?"

"I didn't bother my head about it. Life was dull enough, goodness knows. You read about silly women trying to make themselves important over trifles, and I thought she was one of them."

"You regard two murders as trifles, do you?" Findon butted in.

Alison Sidley gave him a cold glance. "Everyone who gets murdered must have been known to somebody, young man. What could my half-sister have had to contribute when she hadn't seen them for over thirty years? Just a load of rubbish, in my opinion."

Richard intervened. "So it's logical to assume, is it not, that what Miss Clare was going to tell us had some connection with their youth?"

"I've no idea."

"Don't start that again!" he said sharply. "Tell me about this school. Where was it?"

"I don't know..." Alison quickly eyed both policemen and went on, "I really don't know except that it was somewhere in France... If I ever knew where, I've forgotten. I never wrote to her. She wrote to father, but I didn't read the letters. I had an ordinary, secondary school education myself, so why should I have been interested in her goings-on?"

Because you were as jealous as hell, Richard supplied the answer, but silently.

"So how do you know Mrs. Clayton and Mrs. Marden were at school with her?"

"Because she told me when she read about the murders. It was also the time when she said she'd broken off the friendships because they were in very different circumstances to hers. By that, I took it to mean that they were howling snobs who wouldn't have had any time or use for penniless Clare. She was always a stuck-up girl— daddy's darling! It wouldn't have suited her to be thought of as inferior. Stupid, I call it. They might have been able to help her."

Richard was feeling thoroughly nauseated. Never had he met a more unpleasant female whose veins were most likely filled with venom instead of blood. His brain clicked away furiously. What other questions could he ask? And then it hit him.

"Wait a minute." He groped for the thing which had eluded him. "If your sister had no further dealings with them after the schooldays, how did she recognize them by the names in the paper? Presumably they weren't married at school."

Alison Sidley twisted her hands in her lap, stopped, and looked at Richard with widened eyes.

"Oh, it must have been that American," she finally said.

Richard held his breath then asked quietly. "Which American?" *Perhaps this was where the threads would finally start to untangle.*

"Well, she wasn't American, but she married one. I was wrong when I said Clare broke contact with all her school friends. This girl went to America to live, and I suppose Clare thought it was safe to keep up a correspondence with her. She was never told about the changes in our lives, and it didn't matter because as far as I know she's never been back. It must have been her who told Clare all the news about the others. Like when they got married and to whom—that kind of thing."

Richard felt the first stirring of elation. Out of the corner of his eye, he noticed Findon's fingers moving rapidly over the notebook. He sincerely hoped that Findon was getting everything the woman said down.

"And the letters are still coming?"

"No. They dropped off a few years ago. Clare was finding it increasingly difficult to write, and her stinking pride wouldn't let her tell the woman why. But they did still exchange Christmas and birthday cards."

"Do you have a name and address?"

Alison rose creakily from her straight-backed chair and went across to an old-fashioned bureau. "A stupid sort of name," she muttered. "Why do all Americans have such outlandish names?" She scrabbled about in one of the drawers, came back to her seat with a small address book, and leafed through the pages.

"Here you are. The only one in the K's."

And there it was—Cassy and Kett Kanderhagen, and they had an address in Beverley Hills, California.

Richard couldn't believe his luck. He could contact his friend in the L.A. Police and get him to check out the Kanderhagen's. Maybe, finally, he was on to some positive lead.

Chapter Seven

"For Christ's sake get me to a pub, Findon, and fast! I need about half a dozen stiff scotches to wash the taste of that old cow out of my mouth!"

"And me, sir," Findon agreed. "But which of us is driving home!"

Richard laughed. "Don't forget we've got to call in at the local nick before that."

In the end, they settled for beer and a Ploughman's lunch—the fresh crusty bread and huge wedge of strong Cheddar cheese going down well. Richard was silent while they ate, and his Sergeant made no move except the chomping of his jaws. Richard went to the bar for a refill of glasses, and when he came back, Findon began talking.

"Where to now, sir?" he asked with a big grin on his face. "California?"

"We should be so lucky! Do you think the Force would shell out for a trip like that to further my investigation?" Then Richard became serious.

"The first thing to do, although I'll admit to you it's grudgingly, is to ask for unobtrusive surveillance on that old, Miss Alison Sidley. Who knows? She could be our next victim."

Findon agreed with Richard, although the look on Findon's face made Richard think that he wouldn't care if she was next!

"I'd give a lot to know how our villain manages to be one jump ahead of us every time."

Findon took a sip from his glass and said, "Do you

think the Sidley woman is involved?"

Richard made a face. "Who knows at this point, but we'd better try and make sure the nasty old specimen doesn't come to a sticky end, too.

I'm glad we brought that address book away with us. Although, I can hardly think the murderer would go haring off to America. Anyway, I've got a plan to sort out that one as soon as we get back home."

He thought for a minute and began again.

"Going back to this question of how the killer seems to know everything we're up to—this is really bugging me, Sergeant, and I haven't had time to think it through properly yet. We blamed Milly for the Marden affair, but who the hell knew about Miss Sidley? A mystery within a mystery, you might say. But I'll tell you one thing—nobody, but nobody, is going to hear about the Kanderhagen angle. I'll have to tell Sir John, of course, but apart from him, we speak to nobody of this. Understood, Sergeant? Not even to your wife."

"That would be a bit difficult," Findon said, looking abashed at the comment. "I'm not married."

"Well, no pillow talk anywhere else," Richard said with a smile.

"What are you going to say at the local nick, sir?"

"As little as possible. Tell them the sister is mystified but should be watched for a while in case of trouble. We'll get away as quickly as we can. I've got things to do back at the house."

As it turned out, they had no bother with the local police. The older Miss Sidley was well known as a constant complainer about everything under the sun, and little sympathy was expressed for her. But they promised to keep a discreet eye on her, just in case.

Richard knew that the head of CID had attained his position in the Force through his ability to solve cases. He had the reputation of being a man who was highly intelligent man and open with all his comrades. Richard was no exception.

"We'll do the routine on this business, Hayward, but quite frankly, I feel we shall only be going through the motions. Something seems to be going on down at your beat, and I'm damn sure you're not telling me all you know. Well, I'll keep in touch and hope you'll do the same with me."

If this goes on, he mused, *I'll soon find myself responsible for solving half the country's murders.* He wondered what openings there were for ex-Detective Chief Inspectors!

Back in his own office, he phoned the Chief Constable. His call was answered after the first ring. *I'm sure he lives by that bloody phone!* Richard thought.

"What news, my boy?"

Richard chose his words carefully. "Look, Sir John. I've a lot to tell you, but I don't want to talk over the phone or in my office. Is there somewhere we could meet privately?"

If Sir John was surprised, he didn't say so. There was a pause before the man replied. "Well, now, you'd better not come here. My wife's got some gossipy women arriving for bridge any minute. How would it be if I drove over to your house? Would you be alone?"

"Only my mother there, sir, but I could shunt her off shopping or something. I'll give you the address and wait for you there."

When Richard walked in the door, Ella jumped up from the kitchen table in surprise. "You're home early son! I'm just getting ready to visit the Claytons."

"Well that's good mum, no need to hurry back, I'm expecting a man any minute for a private interview." *All very satisfactory.*

* * * *

Sir John was fascinated with the house, especially the step-down-in-the-middle of the living room floor, but was too anxious to hear Richard's report for more than a cursory inspection.

He listened quietly while Richard gave a complete account of the day's events. He was stunned by the news of yet a third murder but attached no blame to Richard. After listening to the long narrative, he contemplated, saying, "What's the next move?"

"By the most fantastic stroke of luck, sir, I know a chap in the Los Angeles police department. I won't bore you with details, but he and I worked together closely last year when he was over here on one of his own cases. In fact, he stayed with my wife and me while he was in England, and we've kept in touch ever since he returned to L.A."

Richard continued, "I don't know where Beverly Hills stands in the geography of L.A., but there would be no harm in phoning him, telling him the facts, and asking his advice. Perhaps he could go and see the Kanderhagens—I'll brief him on what questions to ask, of course. And another thing, sir, I feel the Kanderhagen lady should be put on her guard. It seems unthinkable our murderer would go as far as that, but I'm beginning to wonder just how far his hand does stretch."

Sir John was silent for a long moment before he finally responded. "Yes. Phone him by all means, but don't leave the interviewing to him. Go yourself."

"To California?"

"To California. Seems there's no other way we'll ever sort this out. Who is there left now that we know of? Who was at school with those ladies? If we put an advert in the papers, we'd be inviting wholesale murder by what I can make out. No. Your idea to keep this latest information under wraps is a sound one. We'll tell nobody where you're going. You look startled. "

"Well no, sir, of course not. It's just...well. It's going to be a fearfully expensive trip. Er...taxpayers' money and so forth."

"Leave that side of it to me," Sir John said, jumping to his feet and bursting out with a passionate shout, which sat oddly on such a dignified personage. "By God, Hayward, I'd pay for it out of my own pocket, if necessary. This bastard isn't fit to live. First my poor Laura now two other inoffensive ladies. I'd do anything to nail him. It's become a personal challenge now. So make whatever arrangements you can as quickly as possible, and good luck go with you."

* * * *

Richard sat for a few moments to catch his breath when the Chief Constable had left, before he began making a series of phone calls. The first was to Heathrow. A seat was available direct to Los Angeles on a plane leaving at midnight. He booked it, also arranging with airport security to see that his progress to the plane would be smooth and without fuss.

Next he phoned the Clayton home. Alec answered. Richard knew the phone was in the hall so asked straight away if Alec could ensure that nobody was listening. He waited, heard a door close, then Alec's voice.

"All clear. What's up?"

"No details, I'm afraid, but I've got an enormous

favour to ask of you. Could you put my mother up for the night and that abominable dog?"

"Why, surely," came the somewhat surprised reply. "But I'm not allowed to ask any questions?"

"Not at the moment. I have to go away most unexpectedly. I'm sure I'm being overcautious, but I don't fancy the idea of her staying here alone. You have my most grateful thanks."

"The thing is, she's just left us to return home. Would you like me to drive over and fetch her?"

"I'm so much in your debt already—why not plunge deeper? Give us a couple of hours, will you? I'll tell her some tale. I don't suppose I'll be away more than a couple of days."

Alec hesitated as he asked, "Is it to do with mothers' affair?"

"For your ears only, yes, and that's all I'm prepared to say."

After that call, Richard looked at his watch, did some mental arithmetic, and decided to try Harry Cranbrook's home number in Los Angeles. If he wasn't there, his wife would probably know where he could be reached.

The call was booked, and he told the operator it was urgent police business so he hoped there wouldn't be too long a delay. He'd taken the precaution of asking for a supervisor known to him personally. The whole thing would be dealt with discreetly.

While he waited for the call, he packed a small case with a few necessaries. Just as the phone rang, his mother walked in. He picked up the phone and said, "Hold it, please." He faced Ella with a grimace on his face, "Sit down, keep quiet, and close your ears!"

A distinctly American voice boomed in his ear. "Is it

really you, Rich?"

"Harry! Am I pleased to have caught you! I'm in a spot of bother, old lad, and need your help."

"Well! Thanks for asking after the wife and kids," came the sarcastic reply. "Up yours, too! Sorry, sorry, I know how hard up you British are. Guess it's important to be wasting your cash on this call so fire away."

Richard laughed. He always enjoyed Harry's trenchant remarks. "No need to ask about the family. I hope to be seeing you all in person tomorrow."

He looked over at his mother in time to see her mouth drop part way open, and just as she was about to make what he was sure would be a caustic comment, he interrupted.

"To be brief, though. Does Beverly Hills come under your eagle eye?"

"Nowhere near my precinct, this is one helluva big place, Rich. Probably drop your whole county in it and lose it." He relented though. "Okay. Tell me what you want to know. I've got good buddies in Beverley Hills. And what's this about you being here tomorrow?"

"Remember our cash flow, Harry! Not too many explanations now. I'm catching a plane at midnight for L.A., and I'll have to be leaving home shortly. Can you, before I leave, dig up any information about a Kett and Cassy Kanderhagen?" He gave the address.

"Give me your number. I'll get back to you." Nice, short, and sweet, he ended the conversation and hung up the phone.

"What is going on, Richard?" Ella asked. "Where are you off to? Surely that wasn't Harry in California you were talking to?"

Richard sat beside his mother, looking at her worried

face. "Mother," he began in a serious voice. "You and Kate are about the only two people in the world I trust totally. So...yes, that was Harry from Los Angeles, and that's where I'm flying tonight. Now you've got to forget what you heard. Nobody is to know where I've gone—not even the Claytons with whom you'll be staying until I get back."

"With whom I'll what!"

"I rang Alec Clayton just after you left. He'll be fetching you quite shortly before I go."

Ella clasped her hands to her face, looking positively appalled. "Richard! Tomorrow his mother's being buried!"

It was Richard's turn to be ashamed. "Oh Lord! It'd slipped my mind with all I've been through today. But it makes no difference; he's willing to have you, and in fact, you could be a great help to them. It's not going to be an easy day."

"Well," Ella said, "I could take the baby off their hands, I suppose. But why do you want me to go anyway? I'd be quite safe here with my watchdog. I do live alone, you know, when I'm not looking after you!"

"Never mind why—just do as I ask, please. Let's just say I'll feel happier to know you're out of here for a day or so. And remember, if anyone should ask where I am, you don't know. Sergeant Findon might guess, but he'll keep his mouth shut. Now, could you rustle up eggs, bacon, and tea in a hurry? I've not much time."

As he was eating his meal, Richard thought his mother was looking rather bemused and curious, but being a good police mother, she asked no more questions. He would tell her all in his own good time. The scratch meal was eaten hastily, the last mouthful disappearing when the phone rang.

"Harry here. I say, you're moving in high society, aren't you? These Kanderhagens—they're into everything. Oil, real estate, cattle, wineries—you name it, they've got a finger in the pie. Big family, too, and I mean big, literally. Besides the parents, there are three sons, and from what I hear, they make the King Kong look like a midget. Upright, solid citizens, all of them. No whisper of trouble, scandal, or anything. What's with all this?"

"Tell you tomorrow, and in the meanwhile, can you do me another favour? Get someone to keep a weather eye open, particularly on Mrs. Kanderhagen. I'd just like to be sure she's still around when I get there."

Harry let out a bellow of laughter.

"You're kidding, Rich! It'd be easier to get into Fort Knox than their place. They've got electronically operated gates, electrified fences, guard dogs—the works. But I'll pass on the message for what it's worth."

"Grateful thanks, old lad. Where will I find you tomorrow?"

"At L.A. Airport meeting your plane, of course. And another small item—if you don't have time to see about currency, don't bother. I'll stake you for whatever you need, and you can pay me the equivalent when I bring Maryellen over next year for a holiday. Can't wait to find out what all this 'cloak and dagger' business is about."

* * * *

Three murdered women; Fuzz's ridiculous cockeyed bow falling over his eyes; Ella's wistful remark, "Oh, how I should love to go to Hollywood;" all the routine work going on in three separate areas; and Alec Clayton's grief—all these were the stuff of Richard's dreams as he slept his way across the Atlantic. Lastly, thoughts of his darling Kate's shining beauty as she prepared for bed sent him into a deep smiling slumber, until movements awoke him to the realization that they were about to land.

The stewardess, who'd been told of his identity, made sure he was first off the plane. Stumbling slightly, he was on firm ground again and away to the Customs Hall. Here too, he was wafted through with no delay, and there was Harry waiting in exactly the right place, his square jovial face beaming with welcome.

Richard nearly fell over from the force of the warm slap on his back, still groggy on his pins from the long journey. Harry put his arm around Richard steadying him, which turned into a bear hug by both men, showing the genuine friendship existing between them.

"Home to Maryellen, a good soak in the tub, a hot meal, and a few drinks will soon put you right, Rich. Come on."

Richard was surprised to find it was dark outside. He'd forgotten about the time difference between the two countries and how far back in time he'd come. He hadn't altered his watch and had no idea what hour it was.

"It's good to see you, Harry. How much beauty sleep are you losing by coming to ferry me about?"

Harry laughed with the exuberance Richard remembered well. "Nothing to it!" he boasted. "I'm like your Winston Churchill. I can take catnaps anywhere. Did you sleep on the plane?"

"Like a log!"

"Fine. Then we'll be able to have a good natter, as you Brits say. I'm bursting with curiosity, but we'll feed and water you first, get rid of Maryellen, and have our gabfest after."

Richard saw little of Los Angeles as they swept off but was impressed by the bright lights and thousands of people he saw on the streets. "Doesn't anyone go to bed here?" he asked.

"Not so's you'd notice. Always plenty of business for my lot. Crime rate's on the rise, and when the heat waves strike—don't think I ever sleep. Reckon your life's pretty easy going compared to mine."

Richard's smile was wry. At the moment, his own crime wave was quite enough!

He couldn't help staring at the opulence of Harry's apartment—every modern gadget known to man seemed to have its place. "Your crime rate may be on the increase," he joked, "but so's your salary by the look of it. I couldn't afford a pad like this, not by a long chalk."

"All relative," Harry told him. "But meet Maryellen. She's worth every dime I spent on this lot."

Maryellen was a sweetheart—not at all the strident, brassy blonde Richard imagined American females to be.

I must be watching the wrong television programmes, he decided. All the American females I see on T.V. are depicted as blond and buxomly, Richard thought.

"What a great pleasure it is to meet you, Richard at long last. I know you must be tired, so let me show you to the bathroom. Stay as long as you like in the water; the meal can wait. He opted for a cold shower instead, which woke him up and refreshed him. Now he felt ready for anything, including the dinner he could smell cooking.

The talk at the table was all of family matters. Harry was interested to hear all the latest news about Richard's family, as he had met both Kate and Ella when in England investigating a case of his own.

"First thing in the morning, you must send a card to

Kate. She'll wonder what you're doing here, won't she? When's she coming home again?"

Richard slipped past that one quickly, and neither of the Cranbrooks pursued it. He made a hilarious story out of the arrival of Fuzz and his mother's reaction, and the meal went by pleasantly. Maryellen took herself off to bed as soon as she decently could to leave the men to talk business.

With a bottle of bourbon on a small table between them, the men settled to talk. It took quite a while to give Harry the whole story, but he was a good listener and an excellent police officer. He asked few questions but those few were pertinent. Eventually, Richard brought the account to a close.

"So that's why I'm here, and if I get no information from Mrs. Kanderhagen, I think I'll shoot myself! There won't be much point in going home."

Harry looked as if he were considering it from all angles; slapping his hand on the arm of the chair he made a startling suggestion. "I suppose Sir John Thingamabobs' in the clear, is he?"

"The Chief Constable! Good God, man, he's broken up over it. I suspect a love-affair in the past—one-sided, I'm sure. What on earth made you say that?"

"Just wondering where your Mr. X. is getting all his information and so quickly. If this Sir John's okay, and you seem sure he is, how about the rest of the squad? Any rotten apples there?"

This was a new idea.

"Trouble is," Richard confessed, "I know very little about them. My transfer is so recent, as I wrote and told you, and then I was out a while with this bloody leg. But I'll bear it in mind, you can bet your life. I'll go through that lot with a fine tooth comb when I return. At this moment, though, I'm thinking how best to approach the Kanderhagens."

"Ah!" Harry said, looking uncomfortable. "Afraid somebody boobed there."

"Christ!" Richard almost moaned. "Don't tell me something else has gone wrong!"

"You know I told you what big wheels the Kanderhagens are in this neck of the woods? Well, some blabbermouth, trying to curry favour I suspect, told Big Daddy that enquiries were being made about the family from the U.K. He went storming into the Chief of Police, demanding to know what the so-and-so was going on."

"And...?" Richard asked anxiously.

"The big cheese told Mr. K. he had no idea what the purpose of the enquiries was, but he understood someone from England would be coming out to see them. That didn't go down too well, I can tell you, and neither was he happy when he was told they'd been asked to give some protection to his old lady. Afraid that was my blabbermouth, Rich, but I didn't bargain for it getting any further."

"Maybe it's not such a bad thing after all. At least, they're partly prepared for my coming. Don't fret; I don't think any harm's been done. I'll get on the blower first thing in the morning—whenever that is—and humbly request a meeting. You're sure they don't know what it's about?"

"How could they? I didn't know a thing myself till you rolled in."

"Well, can't do any more now. We'll see what tomorrow brings. You might keep your fingers crossed for me."

"I'll do that all right, and I'm also planning to drive you there. It's my day off anyway, so it's no trouble. I'll stay in the car, of course."

"You're a real friend," Richard told him. "I suppose I'd better go and clear it with the local fuzz."

"Like hell you will!" Harry bellowed. "They've had a good tongue-lashing from me already. Let them mind their own god-damn business from here on!"

Richard was amused, thinking how much more efficiently things were arranged at home, but he took Harry's word for it. His friend promised to give him a shout in the morning, and both retired to bed. Richard spent a short time deciding on the best approach before he would phone the Kanderhagen's the next morning. Then he was out like a light.

* * * *.

The Kanderhagen phone number was unlisted, but Harry had it written down. Richard rang, with a slight tremor in the pit of his stomach. He asked for Mr. Kanderhagen, and after a short pause, a man's voice came on the line.

"Kanderhagen here."

"Good morning, sir. My name is Richard Hayward, Detective Chief Inspector, from England. I understand you've been annoyed by my enquiries into your family?"

"Damn right I'm annoyed!" came a roar from the other end. "What the hell's this all about? Why are you taking the trouble to call from England, and what the hell do you want with me?"

Richard's voice was quiet in comparison. "I'm not in England; I'm in Los Angeles. I flew in late last night especially for this. But it's not you I want to talk to; it's your wife."

There was silence at the other end of the line then Mr. Kanderhagen roared out again. "My wife? You're out of your head! My wife hasn't been in the U.K. for—oh, thirty odd years."

"All the same, sir, I demand you let me talk to her. It's vitally important. You can check my credentials with anyone you care to name. I'm staying with a member of the LAPD right now. He knew me in England. Or I can give you a name at Scotland Yard." He was babbling and knew it, but desperation drove him on. Richard hoped that Kett Kanderhagen was a good judge of men, and could recognize the urgency by his voice.

"All right," he said. "Come out to my house. You know where it is? But I insist on being present when you talk to my wife, and if I don't like what's said, I will throw you out. PDQ."

Richard was sweating with relief at the turn of the conversation with Kanderhagen. Harry, who had been listening in, wasn't in much better shape. In spite of their fears, both men ate hearty breakfasts. Before setting out on the journey to Beverley Hills, Richard went for a walk, much interested in all he saw, storing it up to describe to Ella.

California held an inexplicable fascination for her, probably because as a girl, she'd been a film buff, loving to watch any film that was related in slightest way to Hollywood. He knew she thought nothing of present day productions but read everything she could lay her hands on about the old Hollywood days.

Returning from his walk, Richard mentioned his mother's fascination with Hollywood to Harry.

"Maybe we can make time for a trip out to the film studios," Harry suggested. "Your interview isn't going to take all day, and you're certainly not going back till tomorrow at the earliest."

"Depends what I find out, but I must say I don't fancy that flight back too quickly. How these VIP's can practically commute backwards and forwards beats me."

On the trip out, Richard's head swiveled to the left and right then back again like a spectator at Wimbledon. He sent a card to Kate with a message he couldn't resist. "Come home and find out what I'm doing here, my darling."

"I'm taking the quickest route, because I know you want to get this over, but on the way back, we'll go easterly and you can see what the freeways are like. You think you've got traffic problems—wait till you see ours!"

Soon they were in what Harry called Glamour land. "None of these properties are worth less than millions of dollars!" Harry told him as they approached the gates of Kanderhagens's estate.

A guard came out from a small lodge and without opening up asked who they were. He insisted on seeing their official identification which he examined carefully. Richard was subjected to a stare of undisguised curiosity after showing his British Police identification. Only then did the man telephone the main house, and eventually he pressed a button and the gates opened.

It was a long drive, and for most of it, the house was completely invisible. The grounds were laid out immaculately—the lawns unbelievably smooth and green. As they turned the last bend, the house came into view in all its splendor.

Richard gave a low whistle. "How the other half lives! Looks like a film set from one of mothers' beloved old movies, Gone with the Wind or something." The house was huge, gleaming white, with half a dozen wide steps leading up to a covered patio. French windows were all wide open to the sun.

"Yeah! And complete with the lynching party by the look of it," Harry said with a grin.He pointed to the four, very tall, large men standing on the top step. "Looks like the whole family are there to give you the once over."

Richard straightened his back, glad of his own height; at least none of these chaps could look down on him, thank the Lord. He felt at enough of a disadvantage being a foreigner, but the feeling soon left him. His natural arrogance came to his aid. He stepped out of the car and walked up the broad steps. None of the men made a move towards him.

"Good morning. I'm Richard Hayward. Which of you is Mr. Kanderhagen senior?"

A large and distinguished looking man took a step forward and, after the slightest of hesitations, he introduced himself as Kett Kanderhagen and held out his hand which Richard shook.

"These are my sons," he gestured toward the silent three. "We're all here to find out what you want."

Not exactly the warmest of welcomes, but Richard wasn't worried. He was here! "And Mrs. Kanderhagen?" he asked politely.

With a rather grudging shrug of the shoulders, Kett said, "You'd better come in. My wife's waiting for you."

Richard walked into a room about the size of a small cinema, and a lady rose from a chair. He drew a deep breath of pure thankfulness.

At long last he was face to face with one of the original schoolgirls, and she was alive!

Chapter Eight

]
Cassy was a beautiful woman. With his private knowledge, Richard knew she must be on the fifty mark, but from her appearance, could have been much younger. Her clothes would have cost him a year's pay, if not more, and her diamond ring—well, he couldn't begin to imagine how many noughts went on to the figure for that.

The three sons were made in her image all right—with their jet black hair and dark eyes. Richard, before his darling Kate changed his life, had been a connoisseur of women, and he was suspicious of Cassy's raven tresses. *Not even one grey hair?* But the perfect teeth were unquestionably her own, and, praise be, they were showing in a smile.

Taking no notice of her scowling menfolk, she clasped Richard's hand warmly. There was no fear in her face, no suspicion of trouble to come. She spoke, and every syllable of her English accent was still there, proving that she hadn't gone native, as Richard would have put it.

"Welcome to our home, Mr. Hayward, or do I have to call you something else? It's such a mouthful, isn't it? And I'm absolutely dying of curiosity to know what you want with me. But may we offer you a drink or coffee or something?"

"Nothing at all, thank you, and you may call me whatever you like. I'm only too thankful to be talking to you."

"More and more curious," she laughed. "Sit here by

me and start. And you men can stop looming over this poor policeman, or I'll turn you all out."

Richard decided to ignore the men as far as possible and concentrate on Cassy. He plunged straight in. "I've come thousands of miles to talk to you about your schooldays."

All five of Kanderhagens looked thoroughly astonished as well they might. The expression on Kett's face looked like he was dealing with a nutter.

"My...schooldays?"

"To be precise, the time you spent at the finishing school in France. I suppose you'd have considered it an insult to call them 'schooldays'. I beg your pardon."

"But, even so..." Cassy looked bewildered. "You'd better carry on before my husband has you carried off in a straight-jacket."

"You were there, I believe, at the same time as Laura Clayton, Rosemary Marden, and Clare Sidley. I can give you the maiden names of the two former ladies if you require them."

"Not necessary. Go on. I remember them well."

Richard hesitated. This was the difficult part. "I gather you've had no recent news of them, Mrs. Kanderhagen. Within the past fortnight, for instance?"

Cassy was beginning to look faintly worried. "Not for years, never mind a fortnight. The only one of those three I've written to for ages is Clare Sidley and only on birthdays and Christmas. What is this about?"

Richard shot a swift glance at Kett, making a slight motion of his head towards Cassy. Kett was quick on the uptake and moved to Cassy's chair.

"I regret to tell you that all three ladies were murdered within a few days of each other—the first being last Saturday night."

The statement sounded so bald and cold, but there was no way of wrapping it up.

Cassy's face lost some of its colour; her hand flew to her mouth; and shock showed in her eyes. Kett put an arm around her; none of the sons moved, but Richard had a distinct impression of a closing of ranks, perhaps a subconscious protective impulse towards their mother. Kett made for the most important point as far as he was concerned.

"And you think my wife's in danger?"

"I can't be one hundred percent sure of that, sir, but I'd say not. I'm hoping your wife will be able to help me nail the villain."

For the next few hectic minutes, Richard couldn't believe his eyes or his ears. It was like something out of a Western, something he'd be telling his grandchildren about in years to come. But while it was happening it wasn't funny.

Kett sprang to action. He snapped his fingers at his sons, "Boys, get the guns!" Silently they disappeared and quickly returned with wicked little revolvers, one of which was handed to Kett. He was on the phone to the gatehouse giving a rapid succession of orders.

"The gates are not to be opened again until I give the word, not even for the President, the Queen of England, or the Pope!   Let all the dogs go free. Get every man on the estate armed and on constant patrol. Anyone they don't know, jump on him."

He cracked the phone down and turned to Richard, "That man who drove you here, he's an LAPD Officer? Right. One of you boys bring him in here before the dogs are out."

Harry was hustled in and then responded in a sardonic manner. "I guess you've broken the news!" he said to Richard. "When does the shooting start?"

Kett snapped his fingers again. "Drinks for everybody, boys, and then we'll have the rest of the story. What would you like, gentlemen?"

He was as cool and collected as if this was an everyday occurrence. Richard was quite bemused, wondering if all Americans led such extraordinary lives. He noted, however, that while all this was going on, Kett's eyes never left his wife, and the anxious look in them spoke volumes. Obviously, this lady was well-loved.

Kett handed Cassy a drink and sat down with his arm around her. "Are you all right, honey? There's nothing to be afraid of. We're all here to watch over you, and, by God, we shan't leave you for a second."

"Of course I'm not all right," she answered crossly but squeezed his hand and added, "I'm not afraid, either. I know you'd never let anything happen to me, darling."

Kett held her more closely and said to Richard, "Now we'll have it all, blow by blow."

Richard began his story yet again, leaving out no details.

Tears filled Cassy's eyes when she heard the account of Clare's circumstances and the horrid sister. "Why on earth didn't I ever go over to visit her? I could have done so much for her."

"I don't think she'd have let you," Richard told her gently. "You were the only one she kept in touch with simply because you were so far away. She was a proud lady. That fact came from the sister who hadn't a good word for anyone."

Cassy sighed and waited for him to go on. She was

beginning to look ill, and Richard wondered how long it would be before her dominating husband noticed it. Kett didn't miss much. The account wound to its end, and Richard waited for the questions. Inevitably, it was Kett who spoke first.

"That's quite a catalogue of tragedies. I'm beginning to understand why you think the roots lie in the past. But what can my wife possibly do to help? She's told you she hasn't met any of these people for years, and whatever got it going originally must have been sparked off quite recently. Why would the murderer have waited for thirty odd years to begin killing them off?"

"I don't know, Mr. Kanderhagen, but I think you must agree that your wife is the only link I've got with that past. What I really want to know, most desperately, is about this Leslie Pettitt character. Mrs. Kanderhagen, have you ever heard the name before?"

She hesitated, and he could have sworn a spark of acknowledgement was there in the lovely eyes. Excitement filled him.

"No, I haven't." She burst into a storm of sobs and rocked back and forth, clutching her head in both hands.

That was enough for Kett. He picked her up bodily and carried her out of the room, throwing a curt, "Stay there!" to Richard. The three boys followed their parents.

Harry shared a commiserating look with Richard. "Well, you can't win 'em all, pal. Sorry about this." He put a consoling hand on Richard's shoulder, but to his surprise, Richard didn't appear too downcast.

"She knows something! I swear she knows something. There was a—oh, I can't put a finger on it—a look, something, I don't know what. But in spite of Kett's guard dogs, guns, and all the rest of it, I'm not leaving here without talking to her again," Richard said.

Kett eventually entered the room again and before saying a word, poured out more drinks. The sons didn't appear.

"Okay, lets get comfortable," he said, surprisingly mild. "Believe me, I wasn't being a jerk when I carried my wife out of the room. She gets these God awful migraines. Hasn't had one for a long time," with an accusing look at Richard, "so you probably set if off. Guess we won't get into that. Expect you're feeling pretty bad yourself, with all this mess. The bottom line is, when she gets these attacks, she has to take special pills to relieve them. I've just given her one, and she'll be out for a few hours."

Richard could have throttled the man, but he kept his tone respectful when he replied. "I'm very sorry, sir, if I caused your wife's illness, but I wish you hadn't put her under sedation." He went straight into the attack. "You see, Mr. Kanderhagen, I think your wife does know something. Maybe she doesn't even know she knows it, but I believe there's something, and I'll have to dig for it."

He wouldn't have been surprised if Kett had shot him on the spot, but the astonishing man merely took another swig from his glass. "I think you're right. In fact, before Cassy agreed to take her tablet, she made me promise to ask you to come back later on. She wants to recover, and she wants to think, but there's no doubt about it, she's got an idea or two simmering there."

"She didn't mention them to you?" Richard asked eagerly.

"She did not, and there's no use asking me to guess. I didn't even know her in those days."

"What do you suggest, sir?"

"I suggest you go away, do a bit of sightseeing or

something. I won't ask you to hang on here because she'll be out for about six hours. Then she'll need a period to pull herself together, and I shall insist she eat. How about returning this evening after dinner? I shan't even ask you to dine as she won't be feeling chatty. I know the exact progression of these attacks, and this is the best I can offer."

Richard eyed Kett with deep suspicion. "How do I know you'll let me in again once I'm out of the gate?"

Kett gave a barking laugh. "You needn't worry about that. I don't want to be riding shotgun on my wife for the rest of her life. It would drive her mad! No, no, come about nine o'clock. You'll be admitted. I want this cleared up now as much as you do."

Richard and Harry left the Kanderhagen's, grounds feeling the way they did on entering, like prisoners in a compound.

"What a production!" Harry said as they got safely on their way. "Guess you haven't seen anything like this before."

"Can't say I have, but I wish some of our people were as security conscious. It's still the old idea that it'll happen to the other fellow not them. All the same, I wouldn't advocate the keeping of such an arsenal as the Kanderhagens have. Are all those weapons registered?"

A grim-faced Harry answered. "Be thankful, Rich. They aren't so easily come by in your country. Over here you can practically buy 'em with the groceries. Too many trigger-happy fools around. Why, look at that chap back there, he'd have shot a laundryman or postal delivery clerk without turning a hair. You saw his reactions."

"Point taken. Now let's forget the Kanderhagens for a bit. I'm willing to wait for tonight and enjoy myself.

What about this sightseeing you mentioned, or have you got other things more pressing on your day off?"

* * * *

Scrupulously adhering to Kett's suggestion of a nine o'clock rendezvous, although he was itching to be off, Richard arrived punctually with Harry. His previous suspicions were ill-founded, and they were admitted through the gates by a different guard.

The grounds were lit up like the Christmas tree in Trafalgar Square; men could be seen walking round with dogs, fearsome Dobermans, leashed, they were relieved to note. The house itself was a blaze of brilliance from stem to stern, to mix a metaphor. Richard shuddered to imagine what the electricity costs might be.

"Hell's bells!" Richard muttered. "Somebody's birthday?"

Once again, Kett stood at the top of the steps, alone this time.

"Do you realize," Richard whispered hastily to Harry, "I never heard one of the three sons speak one syllable this morning? Are they dumb, do you think?"

"I wouldn't imagine anyone says much when pa's around. He says it all! But don't underestimate them. They're a clever family from what I hear. Dad talks. The boys act!"

By now both men were out of the car, but Harry said he'd stay outside. "I'd like to wander round, maybe have a professional chat to the guards, providing they don't shoot me first!"

Kett overheard and said he'd square it immediately. It was noticeable he didn't urge Harry to enter with Richard. Inside the elegantly furnished entrance hall, Kett halted.

"I'll be frank with you. I didn't want my wife to go ahead with this meeting; I don't think she's sufficiently recovered. But she insisted, so take it easy, will you? And," with a return of his former belligerence, "whether you like it or not, I'm staying while you talk."

Richard acquiesced but was extremely firm on one point. "I must ask you not to interrupt, sir. As you said this morning, you didn't know her in the early days, so there would be no useful contribution you could make. Just hold a watching brief, and I'll be satisfied."

Kett grunted and led the way to a smaller room less magnificent than the one where they'd conducted the previous interview.

He guessed this was Cassy's private sitting room, reminding her of the England she'd left behind. He wondered why she'd never been back.

Cassy sat in a low chair; huge dark glasses protecting her eyes from the light of the one small standard lamp burning behind her. She removed the glasses as Richard approached, and he was startled.

Her makeup was as flawless. Her grooming was as impeccable as the morning's, but there was a subtle change. Tonight, she showed every one of her official years, and Richard felt a quick stab of compassion and guilt.

I'm responsible for this. God! How her family must hate me. But his detective instincts were alerted. Could this be the break through he was searching for?

He enquired after her health and then dove straight in. "You've thought of something!"

"What I'm thinking will sound utterly ridiculous," she began then stopped abruptly. They stared at each other, the same thought apparently hitting them simultaneously.

"Why, that's what..."

"Miss Sidley hinted in her letter," Richard finished. "Come on, Mrs. Kanderhagen. Ridiculous or not, tell me exactly what the two of you had in mind."

Cassy smiled faintly. "Clare was right about another thing. This sure is going to be a long-winded story, and most of it irrelevant, I should guess."

"Nothing's irrelevant in a murder enquiry," Richard assured her. "I've damn little to go on so every detail helps. Say whatever comes into your head, and I'll sort it out later."

Kett broke in to say he'd tape the conversation if Richard thought it would be useful, an offer Richard accepted gratefully. While her husband set the operation up, Cassy scrabbled around in her handbag, found a cigarette, then stared at it in surprise. "I haven't smoked for months. This is another black mark Kett will chalk up against you!"

Kett showed what he thought of that remark by holding out his lighter for her. She lit up, inhaled then stubbed it out again.

"I don't know where to start," she said helplessly.

"Tell me about your first contact with the other girls at the finishing school." Richard suggested. "How many were there? Had any of you known each other before you went or did you meet as strangers?"

Cassy followed his lead, took a deep breath and began again.

"There were six of us, never more, never less. Madame Dubois, the principal, had a very high reputation, and there was always a waiting list if anyone dropped out. But for the record, not that I suppose it matters, I'd like to clear up one point. You've referred once or twice to our 'finishing school', but it wasn't really that in the generally accepted sense. None of us were members of the aristocracy. We weren't being groomed for presentation at Court or any of that stuff."

While she became reflective. Richard waited for her to continue.

"I suppose we came from fairly well-to-do families and were sent to France to learn things like, oh, organizing small dinner parties, managing a household, training maids, getting enough into our silly heads so we could hold our end up in reasonably intelligent conversation. It was expected we'd marry eventually into the same sort of family as our own, and for some reason which escapes me now, it was considered we'd get a better grounding for that sort of life abroad."

The ghost of a sigh escaped her, and it was apparent her mind had gone back in time to those far-off days. A trifle defensively, she said, "You must remember this was the year before the war. Life was different then, a world away. Sorry, I'm waffling, aren't I? None of this can be of any interest to you."

"But it is," Richard assured her warmly. "It's all background material of which I know nothing, remember. I find it fascinating."

"I bet! Like a museum piece!" came the tart rejoinder. Richard was delighted with the flash of spirit she showed. Even Kett grinned.

"Anyway," she resumed more briskly. "I'm coming now to the point you may find useful. One of the reasons we were there was to polish up our schoolgirl French, and in this as in everything else, Madame was a real martinet. We weren't allowed to speak English at all, which we thought was stupid and, of course, were always breaking the rules. What else could you expect with six English girls? Then we found another way to annoy Madame. We'd speak French with atrocious accents—Anglicizing it. We'd say 'silver plate' for 's'il vous plait', 'hors d'oeuvres' we'd pronounce as 'horse's doovers'..."

"'Mercy buckets' for 'merci beaucoup'," was Richard's unexpected contribution.

Cassy laughed aloud. "Oh, you do understand. I thought you'd be sneering at us for being so childish."

"I think all kids go through that silly stage."

"Yes, but we weren't children. We were grown up young ladies, at least in our estimation. I don't think we grew up so fast, though, as they do today."

"To continue...?" Richard prompted.

"Oh yes. Well, one afternoon, the six of us were alone in the salon, plotting a bit of mischief for the next day, nothing wicked—we weren't too badly behaved on the whole. Suddenly Laura, who was the only one facing the door said, 'Quiet, girls. Little pigs have big ears.' We turned, and hovering in the doorway was one of the mistresses. What we didn't see, was Madame Dubois who was behind Mlle. Fernet. She stalked in, face like an iceberg and said, 'In French, if you please, young ladies, even when you're being rude.'"

Cassey adjusted her position and with a wry smile on her face continued. "She was a sarcastic old thing, and we were all a bit in awe of her. All, that is, except Laura who feared nothing and nobody. She said to Madame in a rather insolent tone of voice, 'We were using an old English saying, Madame. I doubt if you've heard it in France.' Madame froze her with one of her most awful looks, 'I wasn't aware there were any English words which have no French equivalent,' she said."

Cassy broke off and turned to face Kett, "Will you mix me a drink, please, darling? I'm getting dry."

Kett looked at her, anxiety written clearly on his face. "Do you think you should, honey? What about your head?"

"Oh, I'm feeling fine. This nice policeman is being so understanding. Give him one as well."

Richard had a strong suspicion that Cassy was putting off an evil moment by creating this small diversion, but he waited patiently while the drink's routine was carried out.

Cassy sipped, sighed, and took up her story.

"Madame said 'Here is your English proverb translated into French. Listen carefully and repeat it after me. 'Les petits cochons ont de grandes oreilles.' Dutifully we repeated it, except for Laura. Her version sounded something like 'Lez Pettitt cushions', etc."

Richard drew a sharp breath. "Lez Pettitt. Leslie Pettitt. Is this the connection?"

"It might be but, of course, there's a lot more to it than that."

Kett looked as interested as Richard. "I should hope so! Carry on, honey."

"Well, for some reason or other, this Lez Pettitt became a sort of catchphrase with us. From then on, anyone we didn't like, the mademoiselle I mentioned, one of the maids who hated us, we called Lez Pettitt, and it stuck. Nobody else knew what we were talking about, but it gave us a bit of harmless fun, specially when we'd address a taxi driver or a disobliging waiter by the name."

She sipped again. "I'm afraid I'll have to digress a bit now into personal history, but if you've still got any patience left after the rigmarole so far, it's necessary."

"All the patience in the world," Richard said kindly. "Take your time."

"My father held a minor post in the Diplomatic Service. Quite suddenly he was posted to Washington, and it seemed like it was going to being a permanent position. Our house was to be sold, and mother was going with him. Well, you can imagine! I wasn't going to be left behind. No way! In the end, they agreed to let me cut short my French education and go, so I left the place rather hurriedly about six months before I should have. Of course, we all promised to write, but it was my poor dear Clare who was the most faithful correspondent."

She paused then said, "I suppose she was the only one who hadn't much else to occupy her mind. I must confess I wasn't the world's greatest letter writer. There was so much going on. And..." with a loving glance at her husband, "...this chap appeared rather rapidly, and then I thought of nothing else."

Richard couldn't stop the surge of jealousy as the fond looks passed between them. *Oh Kate, when are you coming home!*

"But I hadn't quite lost sight of the old days, and I was interested in Clare's news. Of course I haven't kept any of the letters but there were two I must tell you about. They were written years ago, but I've a good memory, and in the middle of all my own activities I puzzled about them. In the first, Clare said something to the effect that they weren't enjoying life any more because they'd now gotten a real Lez Pettitt amongst them, and they hated her."

"Her?" Richard queried.

"Yes, definitely 'her'. Well, quite shortly after that the

balloon went up in Europe. Everyone knew then that war was inevitable. The school closed down, and my friends went home, just in time as it happened, or they might have been stuck in France for the duration. The second letter I had from Clare, the second of interest to you, I mean, was a real puzzler. Unfortunately, some previous letter of hers must have gone astray because I didn't understand a word she was saying, not in this case of yours, I mean. Are you with me so far?"

"I'm still with you," Richard replied fairly truthfully.

"Well, by the time Clare was home in England, she said she wasn't at all sorry to have left the French school. Mainly because of all the dreadful unpleasantness there had been with the wretched Lez Pettitt."

Cassy closed her eyes and said, "Let me concentrate for a minute. I want to try and remember just what she did say."

Richard waited, scarcely breathing. Could this be the clue he'd been searching for since the first murder?

Cassy opened her eyes again and said, "I won't swear it's accurate word for word, but the sense is correct. It was obvious she'd told me about the unpleasantness whatever it was, in one of her letters I never received, because she said something like this...'It all turned out far, far more dreadful than I told you at the time. She was really wicked, and if it hadn't been for the war coming, she would have been found out by everyone besides us. She was luckier than she deserves.' Those were more or less Clare's words, and this I swear to you most solemnly, Mr. Hayward, she finished by saying she thought 'Lez Pettitt would have killed us if she'd found out that we knew!'"

Chapter Nine

Cassy stopped, exhausted by her marathon talking session. As if the movement had been choreographed, all three raised their glasses and drained them. Richard was the first to speak. "Thank God you taped all this, sir. May I ask you to run it through while I make some notes? I've about a hundred questions to ask."

Kett wound the tape back, set it in motion, and refilled the glasses. Richard made frantic notes on the back of an envelope. The tape finished, and he referred to his sprawling handwriting.

"Now, Mrs. Kanderhagen—" he began.

"Hold it!" Kett held up a commanding hand. "How do you feel, precious? Are you well enough to answer this guy's questions?"

"Funnily enough, I feel better now that I've gotten that off my chest, and if I can contribute anything else, I'll be happy. And please call me Cassy, Mr. Hayward. It seems we've known each other forever."

"And my name's Richard," he told her with the charming smile so few people saw. "Now, Cassy, my first question. Would you say Miss Sidley was the hysterical type, prone to exaggeration?"

"Decidedly not! She was about the best balanced of us all."

Kett intervened again. "I know I'm supposed to sit mum and not interfere, but I'd just like to say that my wife is also a well-balanced woman. What's more I can make my own small contribution by verifying that the contents of the last letter are substantially correct as she told it to you. She showed me the letter at the time."

"Did I, Darling?" Cassy glanced up at him. "Why ever did I do that?"

"Because I was interested in everything about you. You were worried over that damned letter and asked what I thought it meant. Not knowing any of the persons involved, I was no help except to try and take your mind off it."

"Excellent," Richard said. "It's always good to have confirmation. Next question. Have you any idea, from what you knew of the inmates or what Miss Sidley wrote, who Lez Pettitt could be?"

Cassy sounded regretful. "None whatever. I thought about it a lot at the time but couldn't imagine who she was talking about. I'm sure she told me in one or more of the letters I didn't get."

"But you're sure in your own mind it was a girl or a woman?"

"Definitely sure of that!"

"So my sergeant was right but for the wrong reasons," Richard mused. They didn't ask what he meant but waited for the next questions.

"I'd like a run-down on the six girls. You said six, I believe. Who they were and what happened to them when they left France, if you know?"

"That won't take long," Cassy replied sadly. "Laura, Ros, and Clare are dead, as you know. I'm here, but I presume you don't suspect me! The fifth girl, Diane Halland, is also dead as she was killed in an air-raid. I got all my information about that and about the other two's marriages from Clare when she was still writing. Her letters didn't stop until the late 1950's. They'd been getting fewer and fewer and then it was just cards. Now I know why from what that atrocious sister said."

"And the sixth girl?" Richard prompted.

"The sixth girl, oh, that would have been Sarah Brenchley. Now what happened to her? She married during the war, a naval officer, I believe, or somebody in one of the Services. I think Clare lost touch with her completely because apart from the fact that she married, I don't remember hearing any more about her."

"I'll have to try and track her down pretty damn quick," Richard said, and the implications of that remark sobered them all into silence for a moment.

Kett showed an admirable grasp of essentials. "Would you like to phone any of your people from here?"

Richard was quick to take advantage of the offer. The call was booked but not to Burshill. It was a person-to-person call to Geoffrey Brede at Scotland Yard.

"This won't be long coming through," the autocratic Kett informed him. "My calls have instant priority. I suggest we take a short break until it gets back to us. I don't know about you two, but I'm hungry."

Richard was sure the man wasn't anything of the kind, but their dinner had probably been a travesty of a meal. His thought was for Cassy.

"Do you know, darling," she sounded surprised as she addressed her husband. "I think I am, too. Could you toy with a turkey sandwich, Richard? That's what I fancy. And what about your LAPD friend? Shouldn't he come in?"

Richard would have much preferred to carry on with his questions, but politeness forbade it. A quick call on the house phone elicited the fact that Harry was quite happily sharing beer and hamburgers with the guard on duty at the gate.

While they were eating delicious cold turkey sandwiches with all the trimmings, which appeared as if by magic within minutes of Kett ordering them, Cassy asked him about his home life. He told her far more than he realized and then asked her the question which had been puzzling him.

"Why have you never been back to England? You said you'd been to France, Italy, Switzerland, but never to England."

"Well..." she said doubtfully, her eyes focused on Kett.

"No secret about it," her husband said. "I'm a jealous man. My wife was a beautiful girl, still is in my opinion, and I could never quite believe she'd chosen me. Her parents died out here, and I never wanted Cassy to go back in case she was homesick and wanted to stay. She went along with my idiotic notions, and we've never mentioned it since. Suppose you think I'm a bloody fool?"

Richard's reply was heartfelt. "By God, I don't! I'm in the same boat. My wife's a New Zealander, and I had the same idiotic notions. Unfortunately, though, her father's still there, and Kate had to go when he was taken ill. I'm just hoping she'll come back."

Cassy's gaze was shrewd. "Then you're the bloody fool, if you're worrying about that. She'll be home again, if she's anything like me!"

Richard felt obscurely comforted, and this from a complete stranger!

Dead on cue as they finished the food, the phone rang. Praise be. It was Geoffrey Brede. "Richard? Did they say this call is coming from America, for God's sake? What on earth are you doing there?"

"Yes it is, and don't ask questions. Tell me quickly. Any developments your end?"

"Not a sausage," was the inelegant answer. "And you?"

"Making some progress but more of that when I see you. I want you to do me a favour. It's official and in connection with our joint cases. Got a pen handy? Right. Put down this name, Sarah Brenchley..." he spelled it..."born sometime in 1921 or 22. Find out who she married sometime during the war, probably an officer in one of the Services, and where she is now if it's humanly possible. I know it's a tall order, but if it's not done, she could be number four on the list. You've got far better facilities than we have at Burshill, and what's more, I want it kept quiet at my end for the time being. No more for now. Any questions?"

"They'll wait till I see you. You owe me a pint for this!"

"As many as you can sup if you come up with the information. Hope you don't get a hiccup in your queries!"

They said goodbye and rang off.

"Scotland Yard, eh?" Kett rumbled. "Can't say you're not doing your damndest."

"I seem to have been lumbered with solving the lot, but I'm doing the best I can. Now, may we get back to the grilling?"

Seated in their original chairs, Richard began again. "We seem to have covered the six girls for the time being. Let's start on the staff. This Madame Dubois now. What about her?"

"You can forget her," Cassy replied with a laugh. "If she was still alive, she'd be more than a hundred years old. She's probably prodding Satan with his own

118

pitchfork, not stabbing her former pupils to death."

"Right. I'll scratch her off. What about Mademoiselle...Fernet did you say?"

"Same thing applies, but she'll be in the other place, an inoffensive soul."

"The maid you said hated you?"

"No good. She was dismissed before I left. Anyhow, she was a bit simple, and I don't think your murderer's that."

"What about the rest of the staff? I assume there were other maids, a cook, suchlike?"

"Of course, but they came and went with monotonous regularity. Madame Dubois was too much of a perfectionist. We're not getting very far, are we?" Cassy shifted uneasily in her chair, readjusting her position.

"I didn't think we would in that direction. I'm only clearing away the loose ends to be sure I'm not missing anything. You see, unless she spoke perfect English, our murderess couldn't possibly be a foreigner."

"How come?" Kett wanted to know.

"Because we learned from our enquiries that Laura Clayton hadn't been away from home for at least three months before her death. We know she had a problem because she'd written to Mrs. Marden about L.P. Therefore, she must have met her in Burshill, and if you knew our town, you'd realize that any foreigner would stick out like a sore thumb. Somebody, somewhere, would have commented on it."

Richard could see from the expression on Kett Kanderhagen's face that the man could scarcely credit such parochialism. Cassy, apparently delving into memories of her girlhood, bore Richard out.

"You said the school was closed when the war

started. Have you any idea if it opened again afterwards?"

"I don't know about immediately after the war, but I know it's not there now. When I was in Paris a few years ago I made a little pilgrimage out to look at it. It's reverted to a private house. I didn't meet anyone I knew, but I hardly expected to after all these years."

"You sound like Methuselah!" Kett grumbled. "There are still a few of our advanced age around."

Cassy moved across to where he sat and put an arm around him, with the other hand ruffling his thick mop of graying hair. "I know, darling. I think this is the real reason I don't go back to England. Everyone in Europe seems so much older than we are."

Richard couldn't help getting in a sly dig on behalf of his countrymen. "And don't forget you've got the money to keep you looking young!"

"And don't you forget we work damned hard to earn that money!" was Kett's dry riposte. But his next remark suggested that he relented out of deference to the guest in their house. "You're right in a way. Cassy spends a small fortune on her clothes, face, and hair, although to my way of thinking she looks just as good without them."

Cassy giggled like a schoolgirl. "Really, Kett! Is that a two-edged remark? You'll make Richard blush."

A romantic little interlude, thought Richard, *but not advancing my business!*

Cassy seemed to sense this and straightened. "I'm not really a heartless woman," she said softly. "At the back of my mind I'm grieving for those poor girls. Maybe I'm grieving a bit for me, too. It's my youth that's died with them."

She was lost for a few moments in her thoughts. Richard gave her time to mourn in silence.

Cassy sniffed, wiped her nose delicately on a minute wisp of cambric and lace, and said, "No time for tears now. But before we go on, Richard, although goodness knows what more we can dig up, there's one thing that's bothering me quite a bit. May I put a question to you?"

"Please do. This is a joint effort, isn't it?"

"Well, when you told us about the milk roundsman finding Laura's body, he said her words were 'Leslie Pettitt,' and he was quite sure of them. Laura would never have called our bugbears 'Leslie', nor would any of us. It was always 'Lez'. That was the whole point of the exercise—the awful Anglicized French. What do you make of it? Could it possibly be that we're barking up the wrong tree?"

Richard was adamant. "No, we're not! As a policeman, I know the most remarkable coincidences can occur far more often than people realize, but this would be too much to believe. Everything I've heard makes me absolutely certain we've got the right Pettitt, even if we can't put a name to her yet. Seeing Burt Ferring, the milkman, is high on my list of priorities when I get home. I'll also talk to his wife who was there. I'll even talk to the baby who was practically there!"

"That's good enough for me," Kett said positively. "But where do we go from here? And incidentally, has anybody noticed the time?"

As he finished speaking, the clock chimed midnight.

* * * *

"If you're worried about me, Darling, you needn't," Cassy said. "I never felt more wide awake in my life, and the migraine's quite gone. It'd be ridiculous to stop now."

But for the moment, Richard's mind was elsewhere.

"My God! Poor old Harry. He's on duty in the

morning. I'd forgotten him. If I told him to go home, Mr. Kanderhagen, could you arrange transport back for me?"

Kett suggested a different idea."I think the best thing would be for you both to stop here. He can go to bed. We'll find him the necessaries, and the rest of us keep going. What sort of shift is he on?"

Harry arrived, approved of Kett's suggestion to spend the night, and hurried off to ring his wife.

The three remaining in the room got their second wind. Richard, too, was used to working all hours, Cassy had slept for a good part of the day, and Kett was indestructible.

"Any more drinks?" Kett enquired after Harry departed. "I've got to say, Hayward, I'm curious to know how you're going to proceed now. Seems to me all your leads are being stopped up one by one. What's left?"

"I'm working on it," Richard replied with a smile. "We haven't exhausted all the possibilities yet. Now, Cassy, back to school. Tell me exactly which month of which year you left France?"

"February 1939," she said promptly. "We moved to Washington at the end of February."

"Now think carefully. When you left, what were the people there saying about the war?"

Cassy seemed perplexed by this question and had to consider. "Why nothing, I don't think. I suppose we were too young and silly to bother about it."

"Yes, but you said one of the things you were learning was how to hold your end up in intelligent conversation. You came from homes where such things must have been discussed. I know from my reading that France had its Maginot Line. Chamberlain had brought back his bit of paper with, 'Peace in our Time' on it. The war was on everyone's mind in 1938 not just for the politicians. So why didn't any of you talk about it in 1939?"

"I seem to remember." Cassy looked up, reaching back into her past, "right at the beginning of my time there, one of the girls saying something about if the war had come, we wouldn't have had to put up with bossy old Madame. It was a joke and certainly didn't start any deep discussion, but that's about all."

"Did Madame or any of the other mistresses talk about politics or the possibility of war?"

"Oh, heavens no!" Cassy said the words so vehemently there was no doubting her sincerity. "As far as they were concerned, the trouble was all over. There wasn't going to be any war. The English Prime Minister had said so and they'd got their impregnable Maginot Line as you said."

"Why," she continued enthusiastically, "I know Madame never thought it would come because in January they had a great stock-taking. Madame made a huge production of ordering her stationery supplies, books, and etcetera for another year. Apparently it was an annual upheaval."

Richard drew a great breath. "Thank you. That's precisely what I wanted to know!"

Cassy's face contorted with confusion. "I don't see...what can you...good heavens! We're not moving into cloak and dagger country, are we? Spies and what not?" She sounded incredulous, half laughing.

"No...at least, I hope not. But I'm well satisfied with that last bit of information. Now we can start to look for the seventh girl."

"The seventh girl? Whatever do you mean?"

"Think back to the tape," Richard suggested. "Your

words were, 'six girls, never more, never less,' and that Madame's reputation was so good she had a waiting list if anyone dropped out. If Madame was so sure there would be no war, she'd set about filling your vacancy as soon as she knew you were going. Somebody took your place."

Cassy's eyes were brilliant with excitement. "Of course!" she breathed. "Why on earth didn't I think of that?"

"Another extract from the tape," he went on. "In the first of your friend, Clare's, relevant letters, she said something like 'We've now got a real Lez Pettitt amongst us, and we hate her.' Doesn't that suggest she was a newcomer, none of the people you'd known? I'm banking on it being the seventh girl."

"You're a very clever young man," Cassy said, her voice holding admiration as she looked at Kett for confirmation.

That gentleman's comment was less extreme but satisfied Richard. "You don't miss much, do you, lad?"

"Elementary, my dear Watson!" Richard grinned and then wondered if this American knew his Sherlock Holmes.

Cassy's face fell. "But even if you're right, and I'm quite sure you are, how are you ever going to trace her?"

"Because you're going to help me," Richard said with a supreme confidence he was far from feeling at that particular moment.

"But I don't know!" she wailed. "Truly I don't. I told you some letters were lost."

"Or abstracted before they ever got to the post," Richard replied thoughtfully.

"Then thank the good Lord they'd have been addressed to Washington in Cassy's maiden name," Kett retorted. "Or I'd be more worried than I already am."

"How else can I help?" Cassy asked, ignoring her husband's outburst.

"Madame Dubois for a start. Had she any relations?"

"No husband or children but a sister who took charge of the housekeeping. Only she was older than Madame, so she's out."

"Had this sister any children?"

"I don't know. I never heard of any."

"And her name?"

"Madame Pichon."

Richard wrote a note."Now the full name and address of the school, please."

Cassy gave it and that went down. Richard then asked for the names of any of the staff she could remember, but here Cassy was no help.

"We only knew them by their Christian names."

"Never mind. Let me write them down." He did so then added, "You say the town was near Paris. Was it a big town, small town, village, what sort of place?"

"A small country town, not much going on to amuse us. We used to go into Paris for the museums or buildings of historic interest. As far as I recall, there was only one cinema in our little dump. We lived almost like nuns."

"What will you do next?" she asked when he'd stowed his papers away in his wallet.

"Take myself off to France, I shouldn't wonder." Richard laughed. "After being allowed to come all this way off my regular beat, France should be chicken feed."

"But it was all so long ago. Who'd know anything now?"

"You'd be surprised. As your husband said, you're not Methuselah. If it's a small town, there'll be hundreds of people who'll remember the school, especially with Madame's high reputation. It would have been quite well known. Also, there may even be members of the police there who'll have something useful to tell me."

"I doubt that. Don't you remember Clare said they were the only ones who knew what the girl did?"

"Yes, but it's not the same thing. The gendarmerie may not know who did whatever it was she did, but if it was as dreadful as your Clare said, a real crime of some kind, they'd have known about that."

"After all this time?" Cassy asked doubtfully.

"Police work is much the same in all civilized countries. Unsolved crimes are never taken off the files. They may go into a 'Dead End' drawer, but they'll be there. Luckily, Paris and its environ weren't bombed, so even if they have to blow the dust of ages off them, I'll ferret out something."

Chapter Ten

Richard could scarcely believe he was eating his breakfast once again at his own home after a solid ten hours of dreamless sleep. Fuzz sat beside him, waiting hopefully for any small tidbits he might receive. Richard had managed to get into the house without being seen and hadn't as yet phoned anybody except his mother to say he was back. Let it all wait for a while until he was ready to face the world again. Ella was home when he arrived.

Farewells from the Kanderhagens had been most cordial on both sides. He tried to express his gratitude for their hospitality and help, but it was brushed to one side. The only return they demanded was that he keep them informed of any progress made.

He was much touched by the gift of a small Dresden figurine which Cassy's sharp eyes had obviously noticed him admiring. "A present for your Kate when she comes home," she'd said.

Kett unbent with a will, shaking Richard's hand painfully and promising that at long last he'd bring his wife to England on a visit when the murders were cleared up. He seemed to have no doubt they would be. Richard wished he felt as sanguine.

Richard knew his mother would have dearly loved to hear all about everything but wisely refrained from asking him any questions. He would tell her some time.

She was thrilled to pieces with her Hollywood souvenirs and said she'd loved her short stay with the

Claytons but gave no details of the funeral. That too could wait. Everything could wait until he had caught up on his sleep. Which he'd done with a vengeance and now felt ready for anything.

He was on his third cup of coffee when he finally noticed Ella. She was pottering about in a flowered apron clearing the breakfast dishes. Good God! She could only be a couple of years older than Cassy Kanderhagen, but what a difference between the two women—Cassy, elegant, sophisticated, gowned by French couturiers; Ella, unobtrusively dressed, who'd never used mascara, eye shadow, or blushers in her life.

A long-forgotten line of Kipling's came into his mind, and he murmured it half under his breath. 'The Colonel's lady and Judy O'Grady are sisters under the skin!'.

Ella looked at him. "What brought that on?"

"Just thinking I'd rather have you for a mother than anyone else I know." He bowed to her with a smile.

She flushed with pleasure, and Richard was struck with another thought. "Mother! Stop fluffing about for a minute and sit down."

Obediently she sat.

"Do you remember when I was young you had a saying, 'Serious talking time, boy' you'd say, and I knew I'd got to sit up and take notice?"

"I remember."

"Well, the position's reversed. I'm saying, 'serious talking time' to you."

As concisely as possible and leaving out what he called the 'twiddly bits', Richard told her Cassy's story. Ella listened without interruption, waiting for whatever else he wanted to add.

"Now, let me have a woman's point of view. Can you

imagine yourself, at your age, committing murder?"

"Certainly I can!" was the surprising answer.

"For what reason?"

"If I saw you being clobbered by one of your villains I'd, oh, I'd hit him with a hammer or stick a bread-knife in his back."

Richard laughed, trying to picture his peace-loving mother going berserk with a knife. "Fair enough, but that's not quite the sort of thing I had in mind. Anything else?"

Ella pursed her lips. "I get terribly angry when I read about a child-batterer or someone ill-treating an animal. I really believe, if I met that person, I'd do him or her a serious mischief."

"From what I've learned of my murdered ladies, they all led the most blameless lives, and I can't see them going in for those tricks, so your reasons so far are all non-starters. Come on, Mother, think some more."

"Yes, but we aren't concerned with what they were like recently. Whatever happened must have been when they were at that school."

Richard was impatient. "Thank you, but I've already worked that out for myself. So what could a young girl do so terrible that thirty years later she sets about killing all the people who knew of it? What would a woman kill to keep secret after all that time?"

"Well, back in my younger days, it could have been several things. An affair with a married man? An illegitimate child? Maybe caught stealing?"

Richard wasn't impressed. "Adultery? The odd child born out of wedlock here or there? Shoplifting? Good God! Half the population's at it. If it led to murder, we'd be working forty eight hours a day instead of the usual twenty-four."

"Yes, but you're forgetting the generation gap. What may seem commonplace to your lot was a serious disgrace in my day."

"I'm not convinced. You're talking as if you were born a Victorian. What about the bright young things of the 1930's? They were already into drugs and promiscuity. Moral standards were dropping even before the war."

"True, but mostly with the upper-classes of society. They didn't care what was said about them, but if people in my circle did such things, we'd have felt disgraced and degraded if we were found out. We'd have been outcasts. These ladies of yours—which section do you think they came from?"

Richard thought back to Cassy's description. "Sort of betwixt and between, I suppose. Any little faux pas such as you've mentioned would have been discreetly hushed up. But I shouldn't have thought it would matter a damn if they came to light today. This generation has different values."

Ella was prompt to rid his mind of that idea. "There you are, you see. We're back to the generation gap. I can tell you this, my lad, if I'd done anything naughty, I'd go to any lengths to keep it from you."

Richard conceded the point. "But, murder! No, I can't believe you'd go to those lengths, Mother. Besides, you know damn well I'd forgive you anything."

They both sat, pondering silently. Ella said, "I'm not contributing much to your thinking, am I?"

"Yes and no," was his distracted answer. "I understand what you're trying to point out, about the difference in values, but I still can't fathom out why it's taken so long to blow up. Why now?"

"I should say because the murderer is now a highly respected member of the community, a pillar of a society, regular churchgoer, and all the rest of it. She's killing to preserve her reputation, of course. Things nobody would think twice about today would be important to a woman of her generation, don't you see?"

Richard felt the anger rise up within him. "If I discover she's done in all these ladies because they saw her pinch a penny bun from a baker's I'll...I'll strangle the old cow with my own hands!"

Ella laughed. "I believe you would at that. Don't they say we've all got a potential for murder inside us?"

Richard's brain was ticking over sweetly now.

"Another fact's obvious. She must have been miles away from those girls for years, probably never gave them a thought. Then suddenly she finds herself in Mrs. Clayton's orbit, and that's what started the ball rolling. I still think Laura was the catalyst. The other two followed because somebody said a word out of turn, letting her know she had more threats to remove."

He remembered he had some more digging to do on that question. Also, he'd have to see Bert Ferring and spouse. Better make that the first job. A phone call to the dairy brought out the fact that Bert would just about be home, so off went Richard, first advising the Station he was back and where he was going.

The Ferring house wasn't quite so tidy as on his first visit, and a strong smell of baby had taken the place of the lavender furniture polish. Pat Ferring opened the door to him, beamed when he told her his name, and invited him in. Bert was discovered in the act of changing his son's nappy, but far from being embarrassed, he was delighted to show his skill.

"Isn't he a beauty?" he asked Richard after the first greetings.

"Does you credit," Richard said with great diplomacy. Privately he thought the wonder-child about the ugliest he'd ever clapped eyes on, but that was hardly an appropriate comment for the doting parents.

Pat took the baby from her husband, saying that she'd put him down for his sleep and leave the men alone.

"Please come back," Richard said hastily. "I'd like to talk to you both."

Her face clouded for a moment as if she could guess the subject of the talk. She was soon back and sat beside her husband.

Richard began. "I'm sorry to have to remind you of that awful night, but I'd be obliged if you'd go through it once more. You first, Bert. Tell me again exactly what happened."

He wasn't interested in the start of the account, but neither did he want them to know the important part, so he listened patiently to what was substantially the same story as he'd heard before.

Bert arrived at the point where he knelt beside the dying woman. "I said to her, 'What happened? Who did it?' and faint but clear she said 'Leslie Pettitt.'"

"And you'd swear that was the name?"

"I did, didn't I?" Bert asked proudly, "at the inquest."

"Were you called at the inquest, Mrs. Ferring?"

"No need was there? I'd have said the same as Bert. Faint like he said but I heard it. 'Les Pettitt,' she said."

Richard's heart missed a beat, but outwardly there was no change in the quiet voice. "Les or Leslie?"

Pat tossed a defiant look at Bert, who shrugged his shoulders and said, "Les? Leslie? What's the difference?"

"For strict accuracy we should have the exact name. Which was it?"

Pat answered. "As Bert says, it doesn't really matter but I'm sure she said 'Les.' When I argued with him about it, he said it must have been 'Leslie' because a lady like Mrs. Clayton wouldn't shorten names."

"Stands to reason, doesn't it?" Bert asked indignantly. "I bet nobody calls you 'Dick', sir. None of your Charlies or Jacks with people like her. It's always Richard, Charles, or John. It's their way."

"Usually," Richard answered. "But she called you Bert, didn't she? What were you christened? Robert? Hubert?"

"Albert actually," Bert answered thoughtfully. "The wife's right, Chief Inspector. She did say 'Les', but I tidied it up as more respectful to her, like. Anyway, it doesn't matter, does it? Les can't be short for anything but Leslie, so I wasn't perjuring myself, was I?"

Richard assured him it would all come out in the wash. He was quietly jubilant. One more confirmation of one more fact. On impulse, he took a fiver from his wallet and handed it to Pat. "Start the baby's bank account off with that."

Instead of going to the Station, Richard returned home. He wanted to retrieve the precious tape, phone Sir John, and request another private interview. On his way up to the bedroom, he saw his mother sitting sewing curtains. With a grin, he put his head round the door and said, "And did you, Mother?"

Ella was startled. "Did I what?"

"Have affairs and leave a trail of illegitimate children round the country?"

He shut the door smartly, avoiding the look she

threw at him.

In his bedroom he lingered a few moments to look out at the garden. Kate had decided they wouldn't do any digging until they saw what was already there, and he felt a surprising surge of pure joy when he noted a few touches of white and yellow under the big apple tree. They must be investigated when he had more time to spare. He shouted at Fuzz who'd made his own decision that the digging should start now.

Richard realized he was going to miss the little scrap when Ella returned to her own house, but thoughts of that brought thoughts of the Claytons and reminded him of his present duties. Putting the tape in his pocket, he went down the narrow staircase. As he was looking up Sir John's private number, the phone rang. He picked it up. "Hullo?"

"Richard?" came the voice of his Scotland Yard friend, Geoffrey Brede.

"Geoff! This is lucky. I was just on my way out. Well, what news of Sarah Brenchley? Have you traced her?"

"Of course, easiest job in the world."

Richard was a bit surprised at the tone of the reply. The old easy friendliness seemed missing. "Thank God for that. Okay. Where is she, and is she married?"

There was a slight hesitation from the other end and then Geoff Brede spoke with a hint of anger. "What sort of silly beggars games are you playing, Richard?"

Richard was even more surprised. "Game! I'm not playing any games. What are you talking about? Get on with it, for goodness sake!"

The amazement replacing the anger was apparent. "Are you seriously telling me you don't know who she is?"

"Of course I'm sure!" Richard was growing angry now.

"Then I hope you're sitting down because you're in for a shock, old lad. She's Lady Bury, wife of your Chief Constable. They were married in 1943!"

* * * *

After the phone conversation ended, Richard sat staring at nothing for the longest time before he finally gathered his wits about him.

The good, logical brain which had led to Richard Hayward's early promotion began to work. With pen and paper, he wrote down various snippets of conversation dragged out from his memory bank.

First from conversations with Sir John...

'My wife's away.'

'Known Laura since we were both young.'

'Both made very happy marriages, and all four of us the best of friends.'

'She was so good to my wife.'

'I knew most of the people she knew.'

'Rosemary Marden? Yes, her I do know.'

'I met Laura in 1940.'

Then there was Geoffrey Brede's joking remark... 'You'll probably end up arresting your Chief Constable in desperation'."

Harry in Los Angeles saying. 'I suppose your Sir John Thingamabobs' in the clear. Just wondering where Mr. X. Is getting all his information?'

And lastly Cassy Kanderhagen's comment on Sarah Brenchley...'She was the quiet one among us but very nice indeed. No question of her turning into a monster.'

Richard looked at his scribbling, stood up, and walked about the room, thinking hard about his random jottings. Could Sir John? No, preposterous! Unless he was the finest actor the world had ever known, his distress at Laura's death was genuine beyond doubt.

But what about the discrepancies? He studied his notes again. Sir John had said he'd known Laura since they were quite young, but at a later date, when denying any knowledge of the school business, said they hadn't met until about 1940. Well, that was reasonable enough.

Richard didn't know the man's age, but he had to be in his sixties. Nothing necessarily sinister there. But if his wife and Laura were at school together and they'd all met when Mrs. Marden was visiting from South Africa, surely it would have been only natural that some of the talk should have concerned their days in France.

And why, with one of those old school friends, Lady Bury, right on the doorstep, had Laura chosen to confide in the one living thousands of miles away...especially if something criminal had occurred? Sir John should have been the most appropriate person to approach.

Richard's musings brought him round to the most important question of all...why hadn't Sir John told him about his wife...ex-Sarah Brenchley?

Another fragment of a past talk with the man came into his mind... 'Who is there left now that we know of who was at school with those ladies.'

Good God! That was a downright lie! Richard hadn't as yet heard the American tape where her name was mentioned for the first time, but he sure as hell knew this blasted school business was a prime factor in the case he so desperately wanted solved.

What on earth was the blasted man doing? Trying to protect his wife? And what was she thinking about it all? Richard realized he'd never even seen the woman.

Perhaps she was in poor health and her husband was keeping it from her knowledge.

With a sigh of frustration, Richard threw his notes in the fire and watched them burn to the last ash. He'd have to see Sir John, have it out with him, and try to find some answers.

The Chief Constable wasn't stupid, so he'd know as well as Richard that Lady Bury needed protection while this female Borgia was still in the rampage. A thought struck him then. Had Sir John sent his wife away to a safe place?

Well, get it over with. Ring the man right now.

His last question was answered immediately, when a woman's voice came on the line. "Lady Bury speaking."

Richard was taken aback.

"Oh. Er...good morning. Chief Inspector Hayward here. May I speak to Sir John, please?"

"I'm afraid he's out at the moment, but I'm expecting him back in about half an hour. Shall I ask him to ring you?"

Richard thought he'd very much like to meet this elusive lady. "I think, Lady Bury, I'd prefer to meet him in person. I'll come to your house in an hour from now. If this isn't convenient, perhaps he could call me on his return and suggest an alternative time. I'm at home." He gave his number.

"I'll tell him," was the brief reply and that ended the conversation.

Used to making rapid assessments, Richard was disconcerted to find he'd taken an unreasoning dislike to a woman who'd only spoken a few words. He didn't know what he'd expected but there was a coolness in the voice...almost total indifference.

Cassy had described her as quiet but very nice. If that was true, she must surely be feeling concern about her one-time friends. "Blessed if I know what to think!" he said aloud, running his hands through his hair.

Ella came down the stairs after he'd replaced the receiver. "What's going on, Richard? Or aren't you at liberty to tell me? You look like the boy who lost a shilling and found sixpence. Aren't you ever going to work today?"

To prove his independence, Richard sat down, crossed his long legs, and said, "How about some coffee before you turn me out into the street?"

"How about a snack with it. Do you realize its lunch time?"

Richard hadn't because the morning had disappeared. Late getting up, talking to Ella, interview with Bert, then this new aggravation. "Oh Lord," he groaned. "And I told Lady Bury I'd be round in an hour to see her old man. No wonder she sounded a bit off! I'll have something quick."

"Seems to me, Mother, I haven't got a single person left to argue this rotten case with, so you'll have to be my confidant."

"Thanks for that backhand compliment," Ella said dryly.

"You know what I mean, so don't sulk. I'm not even sure how much I can tell Sir John now." And he proceeded to bring his mother up to date with the latest peculiar aspect.

Ella said in amazement. "Well. I'm speechless!" at which Richard raised an eyebrow. "What are you going to say to him?"

"No idea. I've never yet met anyone who had to

reprimand his own Chief Constable for withholding evidence."

"There may be a simple explanation. When you went there on the night of the murder, didn't you say his wife was away?"

"Yes."

"Suppose then she was abroad and only just come home. He might not have told her yet."

"There are such things as phones!"

Ella raised her hand, looking as if she was about to slap him. "You're a mine of information today on current affairs, aren't you? You don't suddenly break into a phone call, saying, 'Oh, by the way, dear, three of your friends have been murdered.' He'd wait until he could be with her to comfort her."

"Fair enough!" Richard replied. "But that shouldn't have stopped him telling me she was one of those original girls. I refuse to believe he doesn't know it. You can't make excuses for him there." He gazed at his watch. "Well, nobody's phoned to cancel my appointment, so I'll be on my way. Just have to play it by ear. Will you buzz the Station and tell them where I'm going? They'll think I've emigrated."

Acting on a sudden impulse which he didn't understand himself, he took the precious tape out of his pocket again and hid it in the bathroom. It would depend on the outcome of the next hour or so what he told Sir John.

This is getting ridiculous, he thought, *when the only person a policemen can confide in is his mother*! He'd suspect his own shadow next if this went on much longer.

While he was driving, Richard tried to plan what he would say, but you can't rehearse speeches without the proper cues, as he soon decided. *Best wait and see.*

Sir John opened the door, looking his usual affable self. "Come in, come in, Hayward. We were just about to have our coffee, so you can join us. This way."

Coffee was the last thing Richard wanted. He was practically swimming in the stuff already, but it would be a good opportunity to see Lady Bury without the embarrassment of asking. Not the cozy study this time but an elegant drawing room, and sitting in it was the woman he wanted to meet.

Sir John made the introductions. "I don't think you've met my wife. My dear, this is Detective Chief Inspector Hayward."

Richard studied her with interest. She must have been around fifty, judging by all the others involved, but had worn well. Not so glamorous as Cassy Kanderhagen, she was well dressed but in clothes suitable to the country woman of substance. Her graying hair had been allowed to stay as nature intended, no pretense with tinting, discreet make-up. There was, however, an air of authority about her as if she knew what was due to her as Lady Bury, wife to the Chief Constable.

"No," Richard said pleasantly. "Lady Bury was away, I believe, when I came here before."

"That's right. My wife has a passion for the Ballet which I don't share, so she takes herself off to Town occasionally where she knows she can enjoy it without knowing I'm bored stiff."

They were all sitting now, Richard with the unwanted cup of coffee in his hand.

"Do you like the Ballet?" Lady Bury enquired conversationally.

"Not particularly," Richard answered in the same

vein, "but I am a music lover, and some of the music written for Ballet is very fine."

What the hell are we sitting around like this for? He queried silently. *Like guests making polite noises at a party.* He'd stop this nonsense.

"I imagine," he said to the lady, "you were pretty upset when you came back to hear about Mrs. Clayton's murder?"

"Yes indeed," she replied. "Quite dreadful. She'll be a great loss to the town."

Richard was nearly startled out of his wits. What a conventional remark, and there was no sorrow or warmth in her tone. As far as she was concerned, that seemed to be the end of the matter.

Sir John broke in. "Now, Hayward, tell me the latest news. I'm anxious to hear about the American trip."

Richard was still looking at Lady Bury and whatever his expression must have been like, Sir John misinterpreted it.

"It's all right. You can speak freely in front of my wife. She knows all about this business, but is the soul of discretion."

This was Richard's cue, and after drawing a deep breath, he took it. "If we're talking of speaking frankly, sir, I have to say I don't think you've been entirely frank with me."

Sir John, in the middle of drinking, nearly choked. His eyebrows rose in astonishment. "What's that you said? What the devil do you mean?"

"I mean, sir," Richard went on steadily, "you didn't see fit to tell me who your wife is—that she was once Miss Sarah Brenchley, one of the girls with whom Mrs. Clayton was at school. In fact," he continued, beginning

141

to feel quite heated, "you deliberately misled me on the subject when you commented that, as far as we knew, the American lady was the only one left of those girls."

He glanced at Lady Bury, on whose face was a cold smile. Sir John, who'd been looking in danger of having an apoplectic fit, suddenly laughed.

"I nearly had you court-marshaled there, young man. Thank your lucky stars. I recollected you're a comparative stranger here. True, I was married to Sarah Brenchley, but she died. This lady is my second wife."

During the ensuing pause, Richard considered several ways of murdering Geoffrey Brede in the most painful and lingering fashion! He might have known there was some simple explanation as Ella had suggested. He decided to treat the tricky situation in as dignified a manner as possible, especially as Lady Bury seemed to be enjoying the prospect of his expected humiliating apology. Bit of a change, he'd say, from the first 'sweet' Lady Bury. He cleared his throat, and then laughed with Sir John who was clearly (thank God!), seeing the funny side of it now.

"I wouldn't have blamed you, sir, if you'd put me back on the beat! My apologies for any temporary embarrassment caused. You may be sure a swift kick in the pants will go to the chap who didn't finish his homework properly."

Lady Bury, whose smile had become slightly sour, poured another cup of coffee for her husband without asking Richard if he wanted one. "Tell me, Chief Inspector," she said in her frigid tones, "who told you about my husband's first wife being Mrs. Clayton's school friend if you didn't already know it? And why on earth should you have thought he would conceal the fact if I were indeed she?"

Richard ignored the first part of the question and answered the second with his charming smile and an attempted touch of gallantry. "I thought the most obvious explanation was his wish to protect you, as would be only natural if a little unethical."

She wasn't mollified although he was blown if he could see why she was annoyed. Jealousy of the first wife?

"But who..." she began again.

Sir John was growing impatient. "Never mind that, my dear. It's been explained, and Hayward is to be congratulated on his efforts, not criticized. Now, my boy, what did you discover from America?"

Chapter Eleven

Richard lied, or, as he would have preferred to call it, bent the truth a bit. He would have had no adequate reason for doing so, if he'd have been asked why at that particular moment. Maybe it was because of the watching, listening woman whose business he didn't consider it to be sitting in on a confidential talk.

"Not a lot, I'm afraid, sir. I had two snags to contend with. One was the fact she's a sick woman and the other was her husband."

"Her husband? How did he come into it?"

"Because he refused to let me interview her alone. In fact, Sir John, he 'took agin me' in a big way for daring to bother her at all." At least that part was true.

"I broke the news to her about the three murders. There was no gentle way of doing it, and I'm afraid it upset her, specially the Miss Sidley one. She seems to have been genuinely devoted to her. She gave me details of life at the French school and names of the only six girls who were there when she was. That's how I came to hear of Sarah Brenchley, the only one not accounted for, and that's why I made it my business to try and trace her present whereabouts."

Richard took a deep breath before continuing. "The result of that, you know. This Cassy Kanderhagen is the only one alive now of the girls who concerned us, and as she's not been to the U.K. for more than twenty years, she'd lost touch with all the rest except for the odd birthday and Christmas cards to Miss Sidley."

"So why did Miss Sidley think she could help us?" Sir John mused.

"We'll never know now quite what she wanted to tell us," Richard answered, with an ambiguity he rather admired.

"Of course you asked her about the mysterious Leslie Pettitt?"

Richard chose his words carefully. "Of course, and that's when things went wrong. I'd left it for the last question, and by this time, she was becoming distressed. I said to her, 'have you ever heard the name Leslie Pettitt?' She thought it over and said, 'No, I've never heard it before.' I was going to push it, but she got hysterical, and Mr. Kanderhagen picked her up in his arms and took her away."

Turning to face the window, Richard said sheepishly, "He was furious with me. When he returned to the room, he told me she was subject to very serious and severe migraines, which could only be helped by tablets of some kind. The long and the short of it is, he'd given her one and that knocked her out. He blamed me for causing it. I didn't win any popularity contests there, I can tell you."

"Didn't she tell you anything of value?" Sir John sounded bitterly disappointed.

Once again Richard hedged. "To tell you the truth, sir, I haven't had a lot of time to sort my impressions. I was pretty well shagged when I got home last night, overslept this morning, went round to have another talk with the milkman, mainly to find out if his wife had anything to add, and then I had the news about Sarah Brenchley being your wife. That's about the sum total of my work today. Of course, I'll do what I can on it, but another unfortunate fact is that even the school doesn't exist anymore. I understand from Mrs. Kanderhagen it closed down when war started."

Evidently it hadn't occurred to the Chief Constable that Richard may have had a second meeting with the Kanderhagens. Praise be. But he was loathe to leave it at that.

"Do you think the American lady will have any further thoughts on the matter?"

"I'm quite sure she'll be in touch if she does, sir. They asked to be kept informed of any progress. But I'm positive she told me all she knew." Which was true, as well!

"The last...the last of those six happy girls." Sir John said sadly. "You don't think she's in any danger, do you?"

Richard could laugh at that one. He described the fortifications at the Kanderhagen home and added, "In addition to guns, armed guards, and dogs all around the grounds, there are four huge men to watch her day and night. I'd be surprised if she's ever allowed out of her own house for years to come."

Lady Bury broke her silence, addressing the Chief Constable and ignoring Richard. "I don't wish to sound pessimistic, John, but it looks as if you've lost this one. I'm beginning to think, as most other people do, that Mrs. Clayton was killed by some mugger. He heard the milkman coming and ran off without taking her bag. I don't understand police work, of course, but that seems the only explanation."

"And what about the other ladies?" Richard couldn't help asking.

She stared at him coolly and pronounced judgment. "I've heard a lot about you, Chief Inspector, from my husband, and I understand you've made quite a name for yourself. Is it possible, do you think, you tend to view these affairs in too complicated a light? A simple mugging is now a mass murder?" The sarcasm was biting. She hadn't finished. "As for the other women, well, coincidences do happen, and I firmly believe these were just that."

She dismissed him, turning to face her husband. "I'm sorry, but I have to say what I think. Naturally you were distressed at the violent end to an old friend, but you've got to try and forget. For my sake, now, will you try?" Her manner was all sweet reasonableness. "Leave this to your people at the Station. Personally, I suspect it will finish up amongst the unsolved crimes."

Do you indeed, my lady! Richard's fury intensified. *Then you don't know me.*

It was obvious to him, the present Lady Bury wanted no reminders of a past she'd had no part in. She was Lady Bury now, and let nobody forget it, including her husband, whose undivided attention and affection should be hers. *Almost as big a bitch as Clare Sidley's sister.* But if this little speech got the Chief Constable out of his hair, it was worth swallowing the insult she'd bestowed upon him.

Sir John, however, wasn't completely under his second wife's thumb. He answered with dignity. "I know you mean well, my dear, and I'm sorry if I've neglected you lately because of this affair. It'll take a long time for me to forget, but perhaps you're right about one thing. I'll leave it to the experts from now on. My last idea wasn't such a good one anyway."

Well, at least something was gained by that. Richard took his leave shortly afterwards, with no acknowledgment except a slight inclination of the head from Lady Bossy boots.

Half way back to Burshill, he pulled into a layby and sat, fathoms deep in thought. Kate had told him once that she fell in love with him because he looked like her private image of the Devil. He had been surprised at the comparison, but in a way, it was true.

In repose, his face bore a saturnine, sardonic expression which had been a great help when dealing with offenders, but the whole effect was merely one of nature's tricks when she fashioned his features. His father had a similar appearance, but in both cases the eyes gave them away with the twinkle which was never far off.

There was no smile in the eyes now. In fact, to a casual observer, he would have presented a grim, forbidding countenance.

His thoughts went back to the recent interview with Sir John and his lady. A detestable woman, he considered her. After about half hour of cogitating, he'd made up his mind on several matters, all of which he started to put in motion when he drove away.

* * * *

His first call when he reached the town was to the public library. There he gathered up two or three books on France and took them into the reading room where he found a secluded corner.

Information about Leveisin was sparse, and the latest volume was only two years old, so he could presume it was reasonably accurate. A small town, as Cassy had said, nothing noteworthy enough to tempt the tourist, although it was only a few miles from Paris. He made some notes, returned the books to their shelves, and went home.

No sooner was he inside the door than Ella came out

to meet him, saying, "All right! I know all about it!"

"Clever old you, what do you know?"

"That Lady Bury is Sir John's second wife. I told you there would be a simple explanation, didn't I?"

"How I loathe people who say 'I told you so!'" Richard smiled. "So now tell me how you found out."

Ella settled for a comfortable gossip, and with a regretful look at the phone, Richard joined her. The next move could wait a few minutes while his mother enjoyed her small triumph.

"From the woman next door of all people. You've met her, haven't you?"

Richard and Kate had collected the keys from next door when they first viewed the funny little house. She had seemed pleasant enough but too chatty for their liking.

Sitting down at the kitchen table, Ella carried on with her story. "I met her when I was coming back with Fuzz from his visit to the vet, and she asked us both in for a cup of tea. It was nowhere near the right time for drinking tea, but I suspect she was hoping for a bit of inside information on Mrs. Clayton's murder. She was full of it. Anyhow, she got nothing out of me, but I took the opportunity to do a little pumping of my own."

"And what did you find out?"

"Well," said Ella, shifting to make room for Fuzz on her lap, "she'd known Mrs. Clayton well. Who didn't, I ask myself?...and happened to mention she'd only met her at some charity dinner a week or so before she died. And when she added that the Chief Constable had also been there and was a great friend of the Claytons, I asked what he was like. That's when I found out about the second wife because she said things were different since his wife died.

Shorn of Richard's hatred 'twiddly bits', Ella's story was quite interesting. Everybody had adored the first lady Bury who, like Mrs. Clayton, had done enormous good in Burshill. They were on committees together and always the first to help those in need."

"I know you think there was a hint of a romance on Sir John's part for Mrs. Clayton, but from what I heard, he was a devoted husband. Then his first wife died a slow, miserable death from cancer, only going into hospital right at the end. Sir John and all of the first Mrs. Bury's friends rallied round to look after her at home where she wanted to be."

The story went on that when she died, Sir John was grief-stricken but tried to hide it by working all hours. In the end, he was on the verge of a breakdown himself, so on the advice of his doctor, he left for an extended round-the-world cruise. He stayed away over a year, and surprised everyone by bringing home another wife.

"Where did he find her?" Richard wanted to know.

"She didn't say, Mrs. Next-door, I mean, so I don't suppose she'd got the details. Anyway, the second Lady Bury isn't liked at all, mainly, I should think, because she doesn't mix. She wouldn't join any of the organizations the first one belonged to, although she was asked out of courtesy."

Ella leaned in to Richard like a conspirator, as Fuzz jumped off her lap. "Poor old Sir John's been made to drop most of his one-time friends, and he's kept on a very tight rope or so next-door says. But how true it is, of course, I don't know. The general opinion seems to be that he married her on the rebound, and she talked a lot of twaddle about moonlit nights on board ship, sort of women's magazine stuff. What did you think of her? Did you see her today?"

"I did, and my opinion of the lady isn't suitable for your ancient ears. I should say there's a great deal of truth in the gossip, but the thought of her canoodling on a tropical, star-filled night would be enough to put me off women for life!"

Ella was going to say something else, but he stopped her hastily. "Sorry, love, but I haven't time to tell you what went on or what an ass I made of myself. You shall hear it sometime, but right now I've got to phone the Station."

He asked for Sergeant Findon who sounded quite relieved to hear him.

"Nice to hear from you, sir."

"Is it?" Richard asked at his dryest. "What are you doing at the moment?"

"Damn all!" was the rueful and truthful answer. "Typed all the reports, helped out on some routine jobs, but nothing on our murder. I was waiting for you to come back from, well, wherever you went, sir."

Richard laughed. "Okay, let's not play silly B's. We both know where I went, but this isn't the time to talk about it. How much longer before you knock off?"

"About an hour to go, sir."

"Right, here's what I want you to do. Drop whatever 'damn all' job you're on and come out to my place. I haven't shown my face in the office all day, and it's a bit late to come in now. Don't worry. I shan't keep you long. I'm just not eager to discuss anything over the phone at present."

Findon arrived at Richard's house in record time.

"You must have been speeding to get here so

quickly!"

Findon hurried into the living room, looking a little embarrassed. "Well sir, I'm quite eager to hear what you have to say."

"It's your day off tomorrow, isn't it?"

"Thank the Lord, yes, sir."

"What do you intend doing?"

"A bit of a lie-in, round of golf if the rain keeps off, a few chores in the afternoon, then taking a rather fanciable female out to dinner and, hopefully, back to my place for a...a chat."

"Ah!" Richard said. "Just what I would have done in my bachelor days off. Now how would you react if I offered you the care of a different fanciable female for the whole day with well cooked meals thrown in as a bonus?"

"Sir?" Findon was confused.

"My mother, Jim."

The Sergeant almost did a 'double take' when he heard his Christian name. The picture on his face was of unaccountable pleasure, although he looked a bit startled at the suggestion.

"I don't understand you, sir."

Richard hesitated, prowled restlessly about the long room, cursing silently each time he forgot the step-in-the-middle. He came to anchor in a chair facing Jim.

"Now listen carefully. I've got to the stage where I'd suspect my own grandmother. You may have heard about my 'unethical' methods, and what I'm doing now is against every rule in the book, so if you'd rather not get involved say so and no hard feelings."

"I'd like to know a little more before I decide, sir."

Richard was far better pleased with this cautious reply than he would have been with an unconditional consent. "Good man! Here we go then. As you've guessed, I went to America. The results of that trip I'm not telling you at this moment because I haven't even told Sir John."

"That surprises you? It'll also show you what I mean by being suspicious of everyone, not," hastily, "that I suspect Sir John. I just feel it's better that nobody should know what I'm up to for a day or so. If I fall flat on my face, I'll do it alone. Now I'm off again very early tomorrow. I won't say where except that it's not to the States. Hopefully, I shall be back tomorrow night. You might even have time for your...'chat' at least. But I don't want to leave my mother here alone for obvious reasons. Are you with me so far?"

"Of course, sir, and I'd like to say now that I'll enjoy my day with Mrs. Hayward."

A charming smile, so seldom seen, lit Richard's face. "I knew you'd agree, but I'm glad it's willingly. When I went away before, I left her in the care of the young Claytons, but she tells me they're leaving Burshill tomorrow. You might be interested to learn they're coming back to live here. Alec Clayton is arranging a transfer so they'll be someone to carry on his mother's house and all she stood for. She would have liked that."

"Indeed she would, sir." A little wistfully, the sergeant asked, "Is that all you're going to tell me?"

"For today it is, but I hope there'll be plenty for you to do if my trip tomorrow goes well. Now, off you shoot, and now leave me to break the news to my mother she's having company tomorrow."

Chapter Twelve

Leveisin proved to be much the same type of small provincial town Richard had expected it to be. Clean, pleasant, unremarkable. With the aid of a guide bought at the Metro station, he made his way to the one police bureau.

Oh what the hell! He'd no intention of disclosing his true identity unless he was forced to. His French was reasonable, and with the help of a pocket dictionary he anticipated no trouble in making himself understood; of course, if he was asked any questions he didn't want to answer he could always plead ignorance of the lingo.

He would have liked to speak with an elderly man, one who might have some slight recollection of prewar days, but the only person to be seen was a youngster sitting behind a counter. Richard addressed him politely.

"Good morning. My name is Richard Hayward, English as you've probably gathered, and I'd like your help."

"Certainly, sir. What is your trouble?"

"Oh, no trouble I assure you." Richard took from his wallet a piece of paper on which he'd printed the name and address of the school. He handed it to the young policeman. "Can you tell me anything about this school?"

His slip of paper was examined with a puzzled frown and returned to him.

"There is no school of that name in the Avenue des Ibis; in fact, there is no school there at all. I know the road well."

"I was afraid that would be your answer, but I know it was there once. Quite certainly before the war and maybe afterwards. Is there anybody here who might remember? I come on very urgent business connected with it."

The policeman was interested and curious but not at all helpful. "Such a person would have to be about fifty or sixty years of age, sir. The war was a long time ago and we have few men as old as that in our ranks."

Richard was tempted to borrow Kett's remark that fifty or sixty didn't quite mean a Methuselah, but he restrained himself and persisted. "I regret to trouble you further, but it is essential that I talk with someone on this matter. There must be many in your town who lived here during the war, but I thought it would save time if I came to you first. However, if you are unable to assist me, I will go to the Mayor."

That brought the young man to his feet quickly. "A moment, sir. I will enquire of a colleague."

He disappeared into an office behind, and Richard heard a quick babble of voices. After not too long of a wait an older man came out, not old enough for Richard's purpose, he thought ruefully. But the second one was keen and shrewd.

"I understand, monsieur, you are enquiring about an establishment which was in Leveisin before the war. May I ask the reason for your interest?"

"There are unusual circumstances and I'm not at liberty to divulge them yet!" Richard replied curtly. "If you can't help me, there's no point in explaining anything, is there?"

"Perhaps monsieur would care to step into my private office, and we can discuss this more thoroughly. I may be able to assist you."

The office smelled abominably of Gauloises, and the slight fog suggested the occupant was a heavy smoker. He gestured Richard to a chair, offered him a cigarette and when it was refused, courteously stubbed out his own which was smoldering in an ashtray. He observed Richard thoughtfully, fingertips lightly pressed together.

"When a foreign gentleman such as yourself comes asking strange questions about schools which do not exist, I ask myself why. This is natural, is it not? I answer myself by saying it must have legal significance. Am I right?"

"I am certainly here on a legal matter," Richard replied. "I would hardly have come especially to Leveisin for a whim. Now will you please tell me immediately where I can go to find my answers? My time is limited. I have to fly back to England today."

The Frenchman continued to eye Richard speculatively. It occurred to Richard later that he never learned the name of this chap. Perhaps he sensed the circumstances were unusual and didn't want to be involved if trouble came of it.

Richard stared back at the Frenchman just as intently. Apparently he satisfied the fellow that he was an upright citizen, thank the Lord, because when the silence broke he got what he wanted.

"Our old Chief of Police..." (at least that's what Richard thought he meant! His French was a little rusty and in general, the French people spoke English reluctantly.) "Now retired, lives a few streets away. He was here right through the war and could probably tell you as much about Leveisin as any man alive. He loves to chat, and I'm sure would be pleased to meet you."

As if by afterthought, he mentioned casually that Pierre Debon was still a good judge of men in spite of his age, and if he chose not to talk to Richard, there was nothing further to be done. Richard thanked him and asked for directions to Debon's house. As he walked out, he saw the Frenchman's hand reach out for the phone.

He'd no doubt this old boy would be warned of his coming and his errand.

The air was sweet and Springlike as Richard stepped out on his walk. He sighed with nostalgia. "Springtime in Paris," he thought. If only he and Kate were there instead of him trotting off to see some ancient grey-bearded man.

The ancient greybeard proved to be a spry, hale seventy-year old, and there was nothing wrong with his intellect or his eyesight as he summed Richard up. Richard was invited into an over furnished room, mercifully smelling of flowers not Gauloises. A brisk white-haired elderly lady shook hands with him and took herself and her knitting away. Evidently another good policeman's wife, well trained.

Debon's first words, after the initial greeting, startled Richard.

"You're one of us, aren't you, young man?"

Richard laughed ruefully. "Is it as obvious as that, sir?"

"I can smell 'em a mile off!" was the equally surprising retort because it was spoken in good colloquial English.

Richard smiled with relief. "Thank goodness for that. Now I can stop inflicting my French on you. Where did you learn English, sir?"

"From one of the teachers at that school you're asking about!"

Richard nearly fell off his chair. Talk about

coincidence! Then he recalled the smallness of the town and realized it wasn't perhaps quite such a miracle after all. "Then I'm really in luck," he said warmly. "You can tell me some things I so badly want to know."

"Not so fast, young man. You'll have to, 'declare your interest', is that the phrase they use? Why weren't our people told you were coming or any questions put by Interpol, for instance? This all seems highly irregular to me. Speak up, boy!"

Richard decided to come clean...well, reasonably so! "You're right, of course. This is all highly irregular." He produced his warrant card for the old man to see. "This is what I am, but I'd better tell you straight out that I'm here without the knowledge, consent, or authority of anybody's but my own. I'm just following a personal hunch."

The old man laughed aloud. "Well said! The sort of thing I'd have done. Are you going to tell me about it?"

Richard considered. He'd have to be very careful now, not give too much away but enough to enlist the old fellow's support.

"With respect, sir, it's too long and complicated a story for now. The gist is this. Three ladies have been murdered within a few days of each other in different parts of England. The only link between them is that they were all pupils at the school in Leveisin between the years of 1938 to 39. From information given me by a fourth lady, another school friend, I believe the roots of these crimes lie in something here. The fourth lady is safe, she lives in America, but none of them had met for many years."

Debon listened carefully then showed the sharpness of his brain. "I've heard and seen enough in my time to feel no amazement at anything. If you're sure of your facts, I believe you. But tell me this, if your theory is accepted, why are you here without official blessing? You said you were acting on a 'personal hunch'. There is a conflict in this I don't understand."

"To be truthful, I don't understand it myself. Had I asked for permission to come here, it would have been granted willingly; every facility available to make the trip easy; my path smoothed with your fellows at this end."

"So you are being extra careful, is that it? You feared, possibly, some other victim might be found in Leveisin? Why? Who would have known, although I think I can guess the answer."

For one insane moment, Richard thought that even this old ex-policeman was going to throw suspicion on poor Sir John. But of course he couldn't; the name hadn't been mentioned.

"So what do you think is the answer?" he asked, really interested in following Debon's reasoning.

Old Pierre laughed and waved his hands in the air.

"Oh, I have no crystal ball, Chief Inspector. I can name no names, but I would guess you're not too happy about someone close to you, perhaps professionally, perhaps privately. But you prefer to keep your actions quiet, is that so?"

"Quite right, sir, but who this person is, I have no idea. It just seems that our murderer knows a little bit too much of what is going on. In fact, I blame myself for one of the deaths. It could have been avoided if I'd take more care."

"Nonsense!" the old man said robustly. "When officers of the law start blaming themselves for the offences of others, it's time they quit! You'll have to toughen up, boy."

Richard smiled. "That's true, and I've never felt this way before. But these victims were elderly ladies who didn't deserve to die. It's gotten under my skin."

"Good, good. Keep a little compassion and don't harden up too much. Now, let me see what I can do to assist."

He went to the door and bellowed, "Louise!" in a stentorian voice. "My wife's a little deaf," he explained to Richard. The old lady appeared, and her husband gave her orders in French. "Coffee, hot and strong, and fresh croissants and butter. Then I wish you to telephone your cousin, Marie. Tell her to get round here immediately. Never mind what she's doing, at once, you understand. And also tell her to bring her diaries for 1938 and 1939 with her."

Richard understood all that well enough; a feeling of excitement was mounting rapidly.

"This cousin Marie," he said eagerly. "Can it be possible...?"

The old man beamed delightedly.

"Yes, and again, yes. Marie, my wife's cousin, is the lady who taught me English and taught at the school you're so interested in."

"But she must be...well, rather old, sir, if that doesn't sound too disrespectful. My informant was sure everybody she knew would be dead."

A finger was wagged admonishingly. "That's the trouble with you youngsters, you think the world began when you were born."

Richard laughed. "Now don't you start, sir. My mother was lecturing me on the same subject a day or so ago. But I understood that Madame Dubois, the Principal,

160

and her assistant, Mlle Fernet, would be about a hundred years old if they were still alive."

"No doubt! That doesn't mean to say there were no younger teachers as well. Marie is about sixty-nine years of age. I suppose you realize there are people still alive who remember the first world war!"

"Of course I do. It's just something I haven't thought about much."

"Ha!" Old Pierre rubbed his hands together in gleeful anticipation. "Well, let us see what two old ones can do to help solve your mystery. I haven't had anything as interesting as this happen for a long while."

* * * *

The feathery-light croissants were almost as piping hot as the excellent coffee, and the lashings of creamy French butter to help them on their way went down a treat. Richard made a thorough pig of himself. He hadn't realized how hungry he was, not surprising as he'd had nothing to eat since an early breakfast.

Sergeant Findon had arrived at the crack of dawn; he and Ella were soon on the best of terms and before he'd been in the house ten minutes it was, "Jim, do this," and "Jim do that!"

As Richard had been leaving, he grinned unkindly and said, "I'll be surprised if you've enough energy left tonight for your-er-chat!" Jim laughed cheerfully.

"It's surprising, sir, where we men can find extra reserves of energy when duty calls!"

His enjoyment of the food didn't make him lose sight of his mission. Wiping the butter from his chin, he said, "I should think it might take quite a while for your cousin to find diaries going back so far."

"Oh, no, it won't." Pierre answered. "A well

organized lady is our Marie. Besides, these are about the only diaries she's ever kept in such detail. There was a special reason, but I'll leave her to tell you about it."

Richard thought he detected a small, mysterious smile hovering over the old boy's face, and he rejoiced. It looked well for the coming meeting.

"While we're waiting, and as I seem to have eaten you out of house and home, perhaps you can tell me if you recall anything out of the ordinary about the school during the relevant years?"

The old man hesitated then said, "I think we'll wait until Marie gets here, and we'll tell our story, such as it is, together. We can jog each other's memories, and you'll have a complete picture."

Richard gave up and asked if he might use the bathroom, which was also becoming an urgent necessity. As he walked back down the stairs from the bathroom, the front door was opened to admit cousin Marie, and he thought idly he could never remember a case before where he seemed to be involved with so many elderly people exclusively.

Cousin Marie was nothing like the roly-poly Louise. She was a tall, gaunt woman, dressed in rather mannish clothing; a shirt blouse, and severe grey skirt.

Richard guessed she paid no attention to current fashion but would always wear the styles which suited her. Altogether she was exactly like a stage caricature of an old-time schoolmarm, the eyes were remarkably bright, and he deduced that nothing much escaped her.

His curiosity was aroused by the two truly enormous books she lugged in with her. Diaries? They look more like company ledgers! Introductions were made; Richard had greeted her courteously in French, and she added,

"Please speak English. I have little chance to practice it these days, and Pierre understands it well enough."

The three of them sat down on the comfortable old-fashioned chairs, and Marie set the ball rolling.

"If you don't want to say you're a policeman, that's all right with me, young man. I like your looks and will help in anyway I can."

Richard almost blushed. "You guessed correctly, Mademoiselle Marie, but I'd rather not tell you the nature of my enquiries just yet. It's important I don't influence your thinking in any way."

She seemed amused. "Nobody's influenced my thinking for years, but I can understand your meaning."

Pierre butted in. "First, Marie, tell him about your diaries. He was a little astonished at the size of them, I think. He knows about the school and will be asking you questions regarding certain aspects of it. I'm not giving anything away, am I, monsieur?"

"Not at all," Richard assured him. "You're both being kindness itself. And," he added, "it would give me great pleasure if you call me Richard. Only my friends are allowed to do that, and I feel I'm truly among friends here."

Richard saw that nothing could have pleased the two old people more. When he switched on the charm, it was like the sun coming out, but he was quite sincere on this occasion. He found, somewhat to his surprise, that there was a great deal more to the elderly citizens he'd met on this case than he'd ever dreamed of.

"To business then," said Marie briskly. "My diaries first, and if I say anything which is not quite clear, ask me for an explanation." There spoke the schoolmistress! "The owner of Les Ibis, the school, was a Madame Dubois who was getting on in years. I joined her staff in the early part of 1938 with an ulterior motive. I'd heard in confidence that she was thinking of selling up, and I wanted to buy. I'd had a handsome legacy from my grandmother, well, it seemed handsome in those days, and it was the dearest wish of my heart to own Les Ibis, which had a very good reputation. I knew all about that, living in Leveisin. So as soon as I attained my position, I began to keep these secret diaries."

She opened one and showed it to Richard. As he'd surmised, they weren't actual diaries at all. She filled in her own dates as she went along. He felt a slight dismay. Written in French, of course, but the writing itself was so thin and spidery, he doubted if he'd ever understand a word.

Marie chuckled. "I know what you're thinking. You'll have to trust me for any translations. But to continue. In these books is written everything I could find out about the day to day running. Budgeting, costing, buying of stock, management of the school, details of the pupils, everything is here. Day by day for 1938 and 1939. It would take weeks for me to read them all to you, so you'll have to tell me which parts are of interest."

She waited while Richard pondered. He tackled it obliquely.

"I was told there were never more than six pupils at a time. Is that correct?"

"Perfectly correct."

"Did they always begin and end at the same time, or were there constant coming and going?"

"They stayed for one year only, and the year began at the end of September. Unless there were unusual circumstances, the same six would start and finish at the same time."

"So you would have had a fresh intake of girls in September 1938?"

"That is so."

"Will you be kind enough then to find the relevant page in your diary and read me what you have about them, mademoiselle?"

She leafed through the pages, saying at the same time, "Please to call me Marie. I know I'm old enough to be your grandmother, but it will save a lot of breath."

Richard replied gallantly that she wasn't as old as all that, but she smiled slightly and didn't answer.

"Right; here we have it. What do you wish me to read?"

"Just the Christian names will do to begin with."

And there they were, his six girls of whom only one still lived. Laura, Clare, Rosemary, Diana, Sarah, and Cassandra.

"Cassandra?" he queried.

"Yes, but she hated her name and was always called Cassy."

"You have a remarkable memory to remember such a small detail."

"It's all written down," she reminded him. "Even that little item is here, but it's true I have a good memory and especially for those two years and those particular girls. You see, if I may intrude a personal note, they were the only ones I ever really knew. The school closed when war began, and there were no other girls to remember. Those who were there when I joined the school, left at the end of their year, and I was too busy sorting myself out to take much notice of them. By the time the six I've just read out arrived, I was ready to take notes and observe them."

"Sounds reasonable. Now, I don't want a complete run-down of everything they did, but can you, either from memory or from reference to your diary, tell me what types of girls they were?"

Without any hesitation at all, Marie's reply came promptly. "They were nice girls, very nice indeed. Oh, they weren't angels, one or two more headstrong than the others, but no real harm in any of them. I'll do a quick flip through and see if anything strikes me. You don't want to give me any leads on what to look for, I take it?"

"None at all. Carry on as you're doing, please."

Evidently Marie knew which pages showed details of the girls; Richard could see that each date was divided into sections, many of them with figures and francs in columns, some with writing only.

As she checked, Marie gave a running commentary; her memory was being jogged. "Laura and Cassy were always the ringleaders in any small mischief, but it was small! Sarah was the quietest, never had much to say for herself but followed the others' lead. Diana much about the same. Rosemary always paired off with Laura if pairing was necessary. Clare was a bit odd-man out, or perhaps I should say rather a fish out of water. I see a note here which runs, 'I don't think Clare Sidley is of quite the same social standing as the rest, but none of the girls let this affect them'. You see, Richard, they were a thoroughly nice bunch."

Marie waited quietly for Richard's next question. He was thinking how well her account tallied with what he'd heard from other sources. His eyes hardened as he remembered how three of them had come to their end.

"The end of September you say was the end of their

year with you. But the end of their September the war had begun. I take it they must have left before then?"

"Oh yes. Any fool could see that war was inevitable, but even so, they left it rather late. I think they all wanted to go together. Let me look. Yes, they didn't get away until August 20."

Cassy was right then. They had just about got out in time.

"And all six of them went on that date?" he asked casually.

"Six girls went but only five of them were the originals. One had left earlier in the year. Now let me think. Was it Diana? I'll look it up."

Richard was dying to tell her which it was and when she'd gone, but he kept quiet.

After a short rummage, she found the entry. "It   was Cassy. She left suddenly in February. Her parents were going to America to live and, of course, she wished to go with them."

"But you said six girls left in August, did you not?"

"Yes. You see, when I said any fool could see war was inevitable, the exception was Madame Dubois. She refused to believe it, and as soon as Cassy deserted us, she sent for a replacement."

"Sent for her?   Did she know her, then, this replacement?"

"Not personally, but there was always a waiting list, and she wrote to the first one on that list asking if she was still interested."

"And I presume she came. What was her name, please?"

To keep up the pretense, Richard had been making meaningless scribbles in a notebook although he hadn't heard anything he didn't already know, as yet.

Outwardly calm. He waited. Was this going to be the murderess?

"Here we are. Marie Westfield, born in London, 1918."

"And what did you think about her? Was she another of your nice girls?"

This time there was a hesitation. Richard's skin prickled. Marie moved her position in the chair and answered.

"To be frank, no. She was not a nice girl at all!"

Chapter Thirteen

"Why do you say that?" Richard asked.

"She was sullen, a mischief maker. She didn't mix with the other girls, and they didn't like her either. She didn't fit in. At first I thought it was just because we all, pupils and staff, missed Cassy who was so popular, but after a short time, I found out that wasn't the whole picture."

"I should like you to read exactly what you wrote about this girl, please."

As he spoke, an odd thing happened. Pierre and Marie glanced at him sharply and then at each other. Richard referred quickly to his notebook as if nothing had occurred.

Marie turned some pages after the entry of the other Marie on the scene.

"This is what I wrote a fortnight later," she said and began to read. 'I hope I may not be misjudging Marie Westfield, but I cannot like her. She had what the English call a chip on the shoulder. Her father, whom she adored, was a doctor, and it was her whole ambition to follow in his footsteps. Sadly for her, he died in tragic circumstances, and there was no money for her to take the necessary training. Her fees at Les Ibis are being paid by a relative..."

"Just a minute, please," Richard interrupted. "How did you discover that?"

"Madame Dubois told me in confidence when I was complaining of the girl's attitude."

"And who was the relative who was paying for her schooling?"

"I'm afraid I don't know. Madame didn't tell me that."

In some strange way, it seemed that all the pretense was over; each of the three people in the room knew it was Marie Westfield who was of interest to Richard. What's more, neither of the French contingents seemed surprised.

Marie appeared thoughtful for a minute and then she spoke with some hesitation. "I don't know if this will help you, Richard, and it's one thing I'm not sure about. But I have a faint memory of being told she was distantly related to one of the girls at the school. Don't ask me which one. It's just a vague something at the back of my mind."

"Your phenomenal memories gone back on you?" Richard teased.

"It must have been a passing remark made by Madame Dubois, if indeed it was really so. I never, to my certain knowledge, heard any of the girls claim kinship with her."

"Are any of the school records still in existence anywhere?" Richard asked.

"None. When war was finally declared, Madame seemed to go a little mad. She'd been getting progressively more eccentric since our troubles began in April, and when the girls had gone, she burned every scrap of material about the school. She said she didn't want it falling into the hands of the Germans. Goodness knows what use she thought the school records would be to Hitler!"

"What troubles?" Richard asked, again with more sharpness than he intended. "But I beg your pardon.

We're taking things out of sequence. You hadn't finished reading your comments on the Westfield girl. Please continue."

"There isn't a great deal more," Marie said, turning again to the invaluable dairy.

"Her fees were being paid by a relative and then I went on, 'but there seems no spark of gratitude in her. She called it charity, I believe. What she really wants to do, now that doctoring is out, is to become a nurse and rise as high as that profession will allow. I imagine that young lady will attain her ambition, but I also have a strong feeling that she'll come to a bad end.'"

Richard sucked in his breath at one point, causing old Pierre to study him closely, but the old man didn't say a word at that moment.

Marie stopped reading and focused on Richard. "There are one or two more entries about her, but if you wish everything to be told in sequence, we can now tell you of the start of our troubles. Both Pierre and I." She faced Pierre. "Shall I begin, and you carry on later?"

"Yes, do it that way, Marie. To begin with, you speak from knowledge. Mine would be only hearsay."

"The troubles began at the start of the month of April. To be brief, a series of thefts. Not from the girls, but from the mistresses, Madame Dubois herself, and even an item or two from the house. Nothing of great value, you understand, and initially there was a feeling some may have been mislaid." Marie paused for breath, and as Cassy had done on a previous occasion, asked if she could have something to drink.

"We'll all have a glass of wine," said Pierre and bustled around getting bottle and glasses.

Richard, while this was going on, had suddenly

become a prey to black despair. What was it he'd said to his mother, 'If I discover she's done in all these ladies because they saw her pinch something, I'll strangle her myself,' or words to that effect. Oh God! Let it not be that trivial!

The wine was poured and sipped, but Richard was too impatient now for the social niceties.

"Is that when you were called in?" he addressed Pierre.

"Not quite yet," the old man said. "Continue, Maire."

"There was some talk of going to the police, but Madame would have no scandal. In one or two cases, she replaced either the stolen articles or their monetary value to keep everyone happy. The girls knew a little of what was going on, but as we didn't tell them directly, they said nothing to us. But it was a different kettle of fish when Clare Sidley lost a pearl necklace. It was quite valuable, a little ostentatious to wear at school, but as I said she was not quite of the same social class as they were. However, when that disappeared, she became extremely distressed. It had belonged to her mother, and the girls rallied round and insisted the police be called upon."

At long last, Pierre's turn had come.

"And not before time, either. As soon as I began my questioning, the staff, both domestic and tutorial, and the girls, I heard about the other robberies, and I was mad. I wanted to know why we hadn't been told about them. Cutting a long story short, we asked all the right questions, we searched the whole place, we asked in the pawn shops, second-hand shops, everywhere. Nothing. Now, Richard, what is the question you would have asked yourself in these circumstances?"

"One of the questions I would have asked myself would be, why weren't the girls robbed first? It would be obvious they'd have more money and probably nicer possessions, if only in the way of underwear which you said had been taken from one of the teachers, so why were they left alone until Clare's necklace went missing?"

"That, too, was my thought. The girls, being young, might not have liked to make a fuss. French people, on the other hand, being thrifty, do not like losing their possessions and would have made a great to-do," he laughed. "I hope you understand I am saying these things with tongue in cheek! But that would have been the thinking of a common sneak-thief in the days before the war, and those are the days we are talking about, yes?"

"I think I understand," Richard said, sounding slightly confused. "Much the same sort of thing my mother was discussing—the generation gap syndrome. But the main point of all this guff, I think, is to say you suspected one of the girls. Right?"

"I have been less than truthful, my friend." Pierre chuckled. "I'm trying to be another Hercule Poirot with his little grey cells blasting away. Actually, the suspicion came when I talked at length with Marie. You see, I was then engaged to her cousin, Louise, so naturally I knew a great deal about the school, more than I should have done. One thing stood out clearly, never had there been any trouble of this kind until the arrival of the new girl. From Marie I knew she was short of money and also had no kind feelings for anyone. She knew the girls would have made a fuss if anything of theirs was stolen which is why she left them alone."

Richard was becoming impatient again. "Sounds reasonable, with your inside knowledge, but could you or did you prove this?"

"I did not. But having exhausted every possibility, I did what I don't think your English police would be allowed to do. I leaned very heavily on the girl, Marie. I showed up at all hours with questions, questions, and more questions. All this, by the way, is written in the diary."

"So what happened? Did you break her down?"

"Not that one! She had the nerve of the devil, but she was becoming angrier. Marie here thinks she was afraid it would come to the ears of the person who was paying for her schooling."

"What did the girls think about this?" Richard asked curiously.

"They, I think the expression is, clammed up. They didn't like her, they stayed silent."

"So?" Richard asked. He was slightly ashamed of himself, but he had a feeling the old man was playing with him, prolonging the anticipation. But anticipation of what? He'd said he was enjoying himself more than he had for years. Well, humour him a little longer.

"Which of us would you prefer to tell the next episode? It's in Marie's diary. She was there, and so was I."

"You tell me, sir, and if I think it necessary, I'll get Marie to read it after." He dropped a gentle hint. "It might be quicker, too. Time is beginning to press."

Pierre took the hint.

"Towards the end of July, I was called by Madame Dubois. Would I go to the school? Miss Westfield had a communication to make. I have to admit that at first I thought my methods had worked, and she was ready to confess. When I arrived, she was in Madame's office; this

Marie was also present. The girl was as cool as a cucumber, a sneering sort of smile on her face the whole while."

Pierre shifted his position, settling back in his chair and continued. "She said she could now tell me who the thief was and named a former maid, Yvette. Her story was that she suspected the girl and had tackled her about it. Yvette confessed, said she was pregnant, and the boy responsible was willing to marry her if she could produce a small dowry. That's why she stole. She had enough; she and the boy were going to Algiers to marry when they arrived. I asked the Westfield girl why she'd kept quiet, and she said she felt sorry for Yvette as she herself knew what it was like to have no money. She finished by saying she let the story out now because Yvette had left for Algiers, and we could stop harassing everybody else."

"And you believed her?"

Pierre and Marie exchanged glances. The old man shrugged his shoulders.

"I made enquiries of Yvette's mother. It was true. The girl was pregnant, and she had left with the boy for Algiers. I asked what money the girl had, and her mother said she had some, but she didn't know how much or where it had come from. When I told her about the accusation of theft, she was shocked and refused to credit it. Of course she would, as would be any mother."

"You haven't answered the question," Richard reminded him. "Did you believe her story?"

"To be honest, I don't know if I did or not. I felt I was prejudiced against the English girl with no reason for being so. The matter was officially closed but then an unexpected thing happened. Marie, your turn."

Marie had been following the story in her diary. She

found the page to verify a date then began to read, quickly, as if she realized the urgency in Richard.

"'On August 15, Madame came into the room where I was giving the girls a lesson. She was highly agitated. Yvette's mother had been to see her; told her the girl had phoned from Marseilles. The boy had left her stranded there with just enough money to get her back. She planned to reach Paris in time for the last train to Leveisin the following day. But Madame, who is showing increasing signs of instability, is afraid of further scandal because Yvette, when told by her mother about the accusation of theft, was furiously indignant, denied the charge completely, and said she would be along to see Madame when she returned to the town.'"

Marie closed her finger on the diary and said to Richard, "That is the relevant part. The rest of the entry concerns my own speculations."

"But Yvette didn't come!" Richard said quietly.

"She didn't come," echoed Marie. "Her body was found in a wooded road, leading from the Metro station to her home."

"How was she killed?" But he knew!

"She was stabbed!"

* * * *

Richard drew a long, sighing breath. He was sure he knew now why the murders had been committed. He knew who the murderer was. But where she was now, that was something to be worked on back at Burshill. Pierre poured more wine, and Richard drained his glass in one gulp, as if it had been a thimbleful of water. The two others waited for him to speak.

"I gather you didn't find the murderer?" he asked.

Again the Gallic shrug of the shoulders. "Consider

the date, August 17, it would have been. The town, the school, the whole country, all in a state of chaos, waiting for the war to commence. Who had time or trouble to worry about a pregnant maidservant who might have been killed by one of the soldiers who were filling Leveisin? We all did out best, of course, but it was hopeless. The girls were packing ready to leave for England. The school was preparing to close down. We had no authority to hold anybody for questioning, much less British subjects."

"But you made enquiries at the school?"

"We did and got nothing. Every one of the girls appeared shocked but still remained curiously silent. They expressed no interest, had no ideas. All were in bed, they said, separate rooms, of course. We know Yvette got off the train at midnight, but nobody saw her after she walked out of the station. And that is the whole of the story."

Richard sat quite still while he thought about the conversation. Pierre and Marie watched him intently. He made his decisions and stood up suddenly; the others followed suit as if on strings. He took both of Marie's hands in his own and held them warmly. "Thank you very much for your great kindness and patience, Marie. One day I hope to be able to tell you the whole story, but for the moment, will you do me one last favour?"

"Anything," she answered simply.

"I'd like you to leave your two diaries here. You'll get them back eventually. Pierre, could these books be put in a safe place under lock and key in case I need them?"

"Of course. I still command great respect at our police station. I'll phone someone to come and pick them up at once. They'll be safe. I assure you."

Marie was beginning to look tired. Pierre, still as chirpy as a cricket, said, "Run along, my girl. Talk to Louise or rest on a bed. I'll call you before Richard leaves."

Obediently she went away. Pierre shouted several rapid orders to his wife then closed both women out. Turning to Richard, he said, "Sit down again. Food is on the way and no arguments. You and I have things to discuss."

Feeling rather weary himself, Richard sat down.

"We have indeed," he said. "And the most urgent at the moment is the question of Marie's safety. I'll explain in a minute, but can you arrange for an eye to be kept on her for a while? I anticipate no danger, but I made that mistake once before, and I'm not taking any more risks."

Without surprise or question, the old man went to his telephone; presumably it was the Police Station he called and commanded that the Chief of Police be with him sometime during the afternoon. Richard was amused as the old fellow still acted as if he was in charge.

"Now, young man!" he began, sitting opposite his guest. "A few explanations, if you please. I'm no dotard, and I now know who you wanted. What has that despicable girl done now?"

"I think she's murdered three of the girls she was at school with. Truly, I can't go into all the details, but I was led to come here because I believed all the trouble began at the school. Everything I've heard today confirms it. You see, my three ladies were stabbed, and that was one of the points which puzzled me most."

Pointing his finger at Pierre for emphasis, Richard elucidated. "For one thing, stabbing isn't usually a woman's crime. They go in for poison as a rule. Secondly, each of my victims was killed by one blow only not repeated thrusts. It was by the sheerest fluke that the first woman lingered a few minutes, possibly only seconds before she died. Long enough to say two words which triggered off this visit. Our doctor told me some people, usually very strong-willed types, subconsciously struggle to stay alive, although there's no medical hope for them. She, apparently, was one such."

Pierre nodded. "I saw you tense when Marie was reading her first account. The girl's father was a doctor. She had the same fanatical ambition to become one also or at least a nurse. Who knows how much she'd already learned about anatomy, for instance?"

"Exactly!" Richard agreed. "That's what I mean about one blow only. A person's got to be sure where to strike to make certain the job's done at once. One murder was actually committed in a hospital; the murderer must have been familiar with the daily routine. The matron there said nobody in a white coat would be questioned, so it looks as if your horrid little acquaintance here achieved her wish, possibly still has her own uniform. With due respect to women in general, they're mostly a backhand lot when it comes to using tools, but our murdering lady knew precisely what she was doing and had the nerve to carry it out."

"With what you've learned today, have you any idea who or where she is?"

In tones which nearly blistered the varnish on the wooden table, Richard answered. "She's your Marie Westfield. By what name she goes under now, I wouldn't know. But by God, I'll find her! Make no mistake about that, my friend!"

"I can see that you are determined to solve this case. You are going to succeed, young man, where I failed all those years ago."

Louise tapped on the door to announce that lunch was ready. How she managed it at such short notice, Richard didn't know, but the meal was delicious. French was spoken throughout, and the old lady was completely captivated by the Hayward charm. He flirted with her outrageously, and she loved it. Pierre beamed at them both.

While one half of his brain was exercising itself remembering sweet nothings in French.

French for his courtship of Kate, the other half was thinking busily of any other questions he could usefully ask. Two things sprang up, which he brought out as they dawdled over coffee and a superb cognac. Marie, who had skipped lunch for a nap, joined them.

"Have you any photographs of the girls?" was one of his questions.

"A few, I think, but they'll be a little faded now. I can easily look them out for you. Not of my namesake, though," she added shrewdly.

"Then we won't bother," Richard replied. The second question was for Pierre. "Can you possibly remember anything about the attitude of the girl when you were making your enquiries after the murder?"

Pierre smiled. "As I had my doubts about her and didn't like her anyway, I watched her closely. She was utterly indifferent to the whole affair. Said, if I remember correctly, that when the war started, she'd go into nursing and no doubt would become intimately acquainted with death. Cold and unfeeling, I thought her then. Seems I was right."

"One more I've just thought of, Marie. Did you suspect any of these girls of going over the wall?" She looked at him doubtfully. He laughed and interpreted. "I mean, slipping out at night when they were supposed to be tucked up in bed."

"I think they did, occasionally, but only by way of a prank. There was no real wickedness in them except for my namesake, God forgive me for saying so. I may have been quite wrong about her. But, yes, it would have been a simple matter for them to get out and in again."

"And yet another!" Richard got up, paced back and forth, and sat down again before putting his hand on his head. "You've said none of the others liked her. What do you think they would have done if they'd known or suspected she'd done something really bad? For instance, what would they have done if they thought she'd killed Yvette?"

Marie was silent for so long he began to think she wasn't going to answer. Then she finally said, "I don't know. If they merely suspected, I think they would have kept quiet. But if they had actual proof she'd done something wrong, I can't believe they'd have remained silent. The problem is to put oneself inside the minds of well-brought up girls of that time. I just don't know how far their code of ethics would stretch. But it's all hypothetical now. In a few days they'd scattered and probably, with the resilience of the young and the excitements of war, they managed to put the experience behind them."

"Did you hear from any of them or anything of them after they left?"

"Not a word," she answered sadly. "We were all caught up in the war and when it ended, it was another world. I never got my own school, just taught in others until I retired, so there were many other youngsters to watch and worry over."

"But you never forgot our English girls?" Richard said.

"No, never. They were...special!"

Richard was thankful he wouldn't be the one to tell her what had happened to some of her 'special girls'. He felt he'd just about exhausted all his questions, not to mention his listeners, and began his long-drawn out departure. They were really sorry to see him go, and he had to promise faithfully to write.

"I'll do better than that," he said. "I'd forgotten the beautiful feel of France. When I get some leave, I'll bring my wife to Paris for a second honeymoon, and we'll come out to see you. Perhaps, also, you'd join us for dinner wherever we stay in that lovely city."

Pierre had one last private word as he insisted on driving Richard to the Metro; said he'd take care of the whole business of the diaries and Marie. Old he might be, he added, but he was capable of that. Richard, of course, believed him.

Back in Paris, he found himself with time on his hands before the plane left. He bought a view card of the Eiffel Tower and wrote on the back, 'How about spending a dirty weekend here with me?' and airmailed it to Kate. It was only after it plopped into the box he wondered if the wording would cause Kate's father another stroke.

He wandered around the shops a while but didn't buy any souvenirs this time. Richard wanted no mementos of this visit displayed around, thank you. *I can't stand all this hanging around!* He wanted to sit quietly and do some serious thinking. And woe betide any hapless fellow traveler who tried to draw him into conversation.

Chapter Fourteen

Richard's spirits lifted when he walked into his own home. There was a tumultuous welcome from Fuzz, resplendent in a new navy and white spotted bow, a more sedate one from his mother, and a cordial "Nice to see you back in one piece, sir," from Findon.

His eyebrows rose into the roots of his hair as he took in Jim's attire—one of Ella's flowered aprons. "Looks as if she's got you well trained," he said and burst into laughter.

Jim was in no way put out. "She has that, sir, and I must say I'm enjoying the experience. I'll gladly mother-sit for you any time."

"Jim has been most kind and helpful," Ella said severely, "so you needn't stand there grinning like a jackass. Now, do you want a drink, food, slippers, or a good hiding?"

"A glass of water and a shower, in that order. Then I'll be halfway human again. I'll fetch the water first."

He went into the kitchen, and Ella trotted after him, half closing the door behind her. From her own apron pocket, she took a letter. "This came by the second post."

His eyes lit up, and he slit open the envelope. From it he took a single, small sheet of notepaper.

"I'll leave you to it." Ella said, walking out of the room, though Richard could see that she was anxious to know the contents of the letter. It was a short note, not much than a few lines.

My dearest policeman,

I haven't been a very good correspondent lately, have I? I've had a lot of things on my mind.

But you can start airing my side of the bed. I'll be home soon. My love to mum and never forget, my darling Richard, I love you.

Kate.

Richard read it twice, stroked it caressingly, folded it carefully, and placed it in his wallet. When he returned to the living-room, Richard could see that the smile on his face warmed his mother's heart. "All's well!" he said briefly. No further words were needed.

"Now, my lad," he addressed Findon. "You've done your duty nobly. Pop off and do whatever you were going to do this evening."

Jim's face fell. "I'm not in a hurry to leave, sir, honestly. Isn't there anything else you want me to do?"

"Isn't there anything I want to tell you, I think you mean," Richard retorted. "Sorry to disappoint you. It's a shameful way to treat you after being such a good soul today, but I'm pooped. I want a quiet evening to sort out my thoughts, and I'll see you tomorrow. I'm off to have my shower, so you can make a nice farewell bow to your slave-driver."

Talk over the dinner table was desultory, mainly conducted by Ella singing the praises of Jim Findon. Richard made appropriate replies, witty and happy ones to ensure his mother all was well.

By the time she'd cleared everything away and

washed up, Richard was sitting by the fire. His mother fetched a book and sat opposite. Richard's thoughts were miles away until he finally roused himself.

"Tell me something, mother. Did you ever resent dad's job?"

Ella closed her book. "At times I did. When he had to work over Christmas, for instance, or had to disappoint us when we'd planned an outing or some such thing. But not often. I knew what he was when I married him. Just as Kate knew with you. Why? Does Kate want you to pack it in?"

"Good God, no!" Richard was startled at the very suggestion and then he laughed. "To be honest, I think she knows I'd hate to do anything else. No, it's not that, but I was sitting here thinking what an odd life we policemen lead. For most of today I've been talking about wicked things, real evil. Now tonight I'm able to switch off and feel thoroughly happy and contented, simply because I've had a letter from my wife. Do you think I'm becoming dehumanized?"

Ella smacked her book down crossly on the arm of her chair. "I sometimes wonder if I gave birth to an idiot!" she said fiercely. "If you want the truth, I find you a bit too sensitive at times. Oh, I know you're tough at work, and most of your subordinates are terrified of you, but you'll have to toughen up more to do your job properly. Of course you're entitled to switch off when you get home, you great booby!"

Richard shouted with laughter and got up to mix drinks for them both. "And I'll tell you something, aged parent. I'm beginning to realize how sensible the people of your generation are. An old boy of seventy gave me much the same advice this morning."

Ella sniffed. "I'm a long way off seventy," she said indignantly. "It's a sign you're knocking on a bit yourself when you admit we aren't all senile. This case must be doing you good."

"Just doing what comes naturally, mum." he said blithely then on came the records—some of the gentler pieces of Debussy.

At 9:30 that evening, the phone rang; Findon was at the other end. "Good evening again, sir. Are you fed, watered, and refreshed?"

"Yes, thanks. What's to do?"

"Maybe something and nothing but I didn't want to make a song and dance in front of your mother. Do you understand me, sir?"

"Understood. Carry on."

Jim's report was brief and factual. "Around midday your phone rang. Mrs. Hayward was at the top of the house, so I answered. A woman asked for you. I said you weren't available and that you'd gone to London. She asked if I knew where you'd be in London, which I thought was a bloody cheek. I said I'd no idea."

Jim lowered his voice. "You'd be dodging about all over the place. Then I had a small brainwave. I said my aunt, Mrs. Hayward, was in and that I was staying a few days with her and Richard—forgive the liberty, sir,—would she like to speak to 'my aunt'. You see, I reckoned if she was a friend or relative, she'd ask questions. She said, no, it didn't matter. I said I'd tell you she'd phoned and what name should I give. But she rang off. She was in a phone box as I heard the money going in. That's all. Could I have done anything else, sir?"

"Couldn't have done better myself. You're a good bloke. The voice now. Young? Old?"

"Difficult to say. It was a well-educated voice—sort of la-de-da. I must read too many soppy thrillers, because I did wonder if she had a handkerchief over her mouth. It was a bit muffled."

"Right. You'd better make out a report in the morning. I hope your floosie isn't listening to this?"

"She didn't show," Jim answered quite cheerfully. "She wasn't interested when the posh meal didn't come first."

"Oh well. Other fish in the sea," Richard told him. "My thanks again."

Jim's tone was a bit mournful again as he asked, "Are we making any progress, sir?"

"Getting nearer," Richard answered. "I'll tell you about it in good time," and rang off.

His mother looked at him enquiringly as he took his seat opposite.

"Wrong number!" he said mischievously.

"So your wrong number's girlfriend didn't turn up," Ella said with satisfaction. "I didn't like the sound of her much when Jim told me about her. Now I wonder who we know..."

"Mother!" Richard said sternly. "Keep your nose out and no matchmaking. There isn't another Kate in the world, so he'll have to find his own second best. Let him have his fling first."

"Like you did, I suppose!" Ella retorted. "Well, it's true reformed rakes make the best husbands, if you're anything to go by, so I won't meddle."

For once, Richard was speechless.

When his mother had gone to bed, Richard inspected all his safety arrangements very carefully indeed. He hadn't much of any great value to interest a burglar, but he practiced what he preached, and his home was well protected, thank goodness.

* * * *

The sun and Richard rose early together in the morning. Moving quietly so that he wouldn't awaken his mother, he walked to the window. It was going to be a lovely day when the air warmed up. The patches of colour in the garden were denser, and there were other colours mixing in with them.

Might even find time to do a bit of digging and weeding, Richard thought, over Easter, and then laughed at himself on two counts. He wouldn't recognize a weed even if it sat up and introduced itself, and what made him think his case would be wrapped up by Easter? The holiday was only about a week away.

He crept downstairs and put the kettle on. First things first, he decided. He'd bathe when his mother was awake, but after a refreshing cuppa', he had a phone call to make. Looking at the clock, he grinned. Serve the blighter right if he got him out of bed. Tea made and drunk, he picked up the phone and dialed. A few minutes went by before a disgruntled Geoffrey Brede answered.

"Good morning, Geoff," Richard greeted him breezily. "What a lovely day to be alive!"

"Oh God, it's you!" was the ungracious reply. "It's the middle of the night, my first day off since the Lord knows when, and you have to be the one to get me out of my pit. Blast your eyes, Richard!"

"They're not the only things about you I've been blasting, either. You and your information about Sarah Brenchley."

Geoffrey's voice was much more alert when he answered that one. "What are you talking about? It was correct, wasn't it?"

"Ha-bloody-ha!" Richard said with heavy sarcasm. "It nearly got me back to pavement-pounding. Your ruddy informant's brain must have gone on strike half way through. There was I, practically accusing my own CC of concealing evidence, and then found out the good lady, although definitely married to him at one time, is dead as a doornail now. Did I have egg on my face!"

"So Wonder-boy boobed," he said. "All right, before you blast me any further, I'll say I'm sorry. As you so rightly said, we only did half a job. Human error. I sent a chap along to Somerset House, and that's what he came back with. I'll kick his teeth in when I see him next."

"Apologies aren't good enough," Richard told him, "and I didn't get you out of bed at this ungodly hour to tear you off a strip. I want another job done."

Geoffrey groaned again. "What the hell sort of outfit are you running down there? One bobby on a bike with a bulls-eye lantern? Isn't there anyone who can read or write and do your own chores?"

Richard's voice sobered. "Jokes are all over now, Geoff. This is damned serious and isn't going to be easy. Also confidential as all-get-out. The woman I want traced now is probably our joint murderer."

Geoffrey was all business then. "Okay. Fire away. Pen and paper to hand."

"Maiden name, Marie Westfield. Born in London 1918. Father was a doctor."

"Yes, got that. Go on."

"That's all I know," Richard confessed.

"Christ Almighty!" Geoff grumbled. "You must know a bit more."

"Well, the rest are probables. At least I know she

isn't dead. It's most likely she became a nurse, possibly rising to Matron. She's the type. I know it was her ambition to be a doctor like her father, so you can check to see if she made it. Nursing schools, training colleges, whatever they're called, that sort of place."

Richard adjusted his position, moving the phone to the other ear. "Might not have been until after the war, but the last thing she was known to have said was that she'd do nursing during the war. Whether she'd have been accepted without qualifications, I don't know. If she just made herself useful, it might not have mattered. In which case it'll be after the war you must begin to look. Oh yes, and to confuse the issue a bit more, she might have changed her name at some stage."

"Thanks a bunch," Geoffrey said bitterly. "When I've done that, what would you like for an encore? Find out who Jack the Ripper was?"

"Deadly serious, Geoff. Until we can find this Lady Macbeth, a few other innocent old ladies might be in danger, including," he added quietly, "my own mother."

That shook Brede. "Right!" he said gravely. "I'll have some breakfast and be on it straight away, but you do realize it may take a while, don't you?"

"Yes, but do your best, old lad. I've a nasty feeling the woman's beginning to crack, and I don't want any more deaths in this case. And, by the way, bring any info to me privately, not the Station."

He rang off, reflecting that he seemed to be gaining a new reputation —that of one who prevented others getting their hard-earned days off. All in a good cause, though—he hoped.

* * * *

Richard had almost finished breakfast when Ella

appeared in her dressing gown.

"I thought I could smell bacon," she said accusingly. "Why didn't you call me?"

"I'm quite capable of doing myself eggs and bacon," he called after her retreating back as she went for another cup.

"And left the kitchen looking like the morning after an Irish wake!" she grumbled.

"Don't worry. I'll send your housemaid, Jim, round to clean up," he grinned at her. "I'm in a bit of a hurry."

"So no cosy chat today," Ella said, half to herself.

Richard sat munching his last piece of toast. "Mother," he said suddenly. "Do you know what a weed looks like?"

"Human or garden?"

"The garden variety. I rather fancy myself out there in wellies doing a spot of grubbing about."

"You'll be about as much use in the garden as your father was," she told him. "Just you leave that to Kate. She said she was looking forward to playing in this one."

"Then we'll do it together," he said, with a besotted smile on his face.

"I'm happy to see you can think of other things besides work."

* * * *

Once he'd arrived at the office, he threw his weight about alarmingly, and everybody jumped nervously wherever he appeared. There were stacks of papers to be signed, routine work to be done on matters other than the murder case, but eventually he called for the Clayton file and settled down to reading every scrap there was.

He knew what he was looking for but didn't find it. Turning his chair to the window, he sat gazing out at the parking lot and a distant view of the hills. Then he rang for Findon.

"I want you to set up two interviews for me," he instructed. "One with Milly Patcham and the second with the vicar and his wife—anytime today."

"Blimey!" Jim said inelegantly. "We're not going to arrest the Reverend, are we?"

"Stranger things have happened, but no. Reading through what we've got, and that's precious little, it seems these two were her closest friends. I'd like a chat with them. Can you take shorthand? Good. Then you can tag along."

Jim reported to Richard later that both Milly and the Amberleys would be at home all afternoon, so they could call at any time. Richard opted to speak with Milly first.

As they drove along the High Street, on a sudden impulse, he asked Findon to stop a minute, dived into a florist's, and came out with a bunch of flowers. *Mother's right about me being a bit soft.*

To Findon he said, "Help to sweeten Milly. She terrifies me!"

Milly's eyes were still red, and it was obvious she hadn't recovered from Laura's death yet. She was touched by the gift of flowers. "Fer me!" she ejaculated. "I 'aven't 'ad flahs given me fer I dunno 'ow long."

"Thought they might cheer you up a bit," Richard said. "May we come in?"

"Where's me manners?" she scolded herself. "Come in me front parlour. Wipe yer boots, mind!"

They sat down on her comfortable chairs, and Milly, having got over her surprise at the flowers, became belligerent. Richard could almost see the arms akimbo in his mind's eye.

"Nah then!" she attacked. "What yer doin' about my poor dear madam's death? Why 'aven't yer caught the bastard yet? Draggin' yer arses is what you're doin'!"

"We're making progress, but I need to ask some more questions about Mrs. Clayton's life here in Burshill."

"Anythin'," she said eagerly. "I'd do anythin' to 'elp. Ask away."

"You knew Mrs. Clayton as well as anyone," Richard flattered her. "Did she go out much in the evenings, socially, I mean, not to meetings and suchlike?"

Milly screwed up her eyes in concentration and took her time to answer.

"Nowhere near as much as she did when 'er 'usband was alive. She used ter say, a woman on 'er own was a liability, I think that was the word, and most of 'er old friends was married couples. She'd go across the Vicarage to dinner once a week and they come 'ere likewise."

She paused, and the ready tears came into her eyes. "Yer know, I never thought about it before, but she must 'ave been real lonely since Mr. Clayton was took. Me now, well, I 'as me mates, and we all go down the pub. I pays me whack, and it's all in together, like. But a lady, no, she couldn't go to no pub." She sighed. "But she read and listened to records. She wrote a lot. She was seckertery to a lot 'o things, and that kept 'er busy."

"Apart from the vicar...?" Richard urged her on.

"She went to a few charity do's, but she wasn't much of a one fer dressin' up. Said she liked 'er own fireside in winter, and in the summer, she'd be out in the garden 'til dusk. She loved that garden."

"Had you heard her mention any newcomer to the town or visitors to the meetings whom she hadn't seen for a long time. Any names you didn't know crop up in your conversations?"

Milly stared at him shrewdly. "Yer don't think it was just some yobbo as killed Mrs. Clayton, do yer? You're lookin' fer somebody else."

"We have to consider all the angles," Richard answered conventionally. "Can you think of anybody?"

Once again her concentration was almost a tangible willing of herself to come up with a name, but the effort failed. "No, I can't," she said regretfully, "and I knows most things as goes on."

Richard rose to his feet, dwarfing Milly who also stood. "Never mind," he said. "Give it a thought now and then, but don't mention it to anyone else." Sternly he added, "This is official business, and I shall come down on you very hard indeed if I hear you've told anyone about our conversation. And I shall hear, you know."

A subdued Milly promised fervently she wouldn't. As she showed them out, she said, "One good thing 'appened. Young Alec's comin' to live in 'er 'ouse with the wife and baby, and they've asked me to do fer 'em. What d'yer think of that now? I'm really 'appy about it."

Privately, Richard thought her choice of words was a bit unfortunate but agreed with her it would indeed be nice for all concerned.

Back in the car, Findon said, "Hope nobody takes it into their heads to 'do' for Milly. D'you think she'll gossip, sir?"

"Not really," Richard answered. "I think the official warning will stop her, and she's not daft, you know. The implications of that chat will sink in, might frighten her a bit, I'm afraid, but let's hope it won't be for long."

* * * *

The first quarter of an hour at the vicarage was both

trying and embarrassing. The Reverend George Amberley would never be quite the same, and all because the unfortunate man suffered with wheezy tubes. He was almost wringing his hands as he moaned over and over again, "If only I'd seen her across the park in the fog."

Nothing consoled him and Richard thought he must be like one of the old martyrs who finished up rejoicing in their martyrdom. Unkind, he admonished himself, but began to get a bit fed up.

"Now, look here, sir," he said loudly, to drown the weeping and wailing and gnashing of teeth. "In my opinion, it would have made no difference if you'd taken her home that night. The murderer would have tried again another time."

That brought both the Reverend and Mrs. Amberley up short; they looked at him in astonishment.

"I don't understand," the bewildered vicar said. "Wasn't it some hooligan who killed her? I'm a man of peace, but I'd have had a go if I'd been with her."

Richard interrupted the flow. "I'm not prepared to give details, and being a clergyman, I expect you to treat this as highly confidential. I know now that Laura Clayton's murder was a personal affair. She was an intended victim, not someone picked at random."

"Impossible!" and "Nonsense!" were the indignant comments.

"Not impossible and not nonsense," Richard went on patiently. "You must take my word for it that it's the truth. Perhaps with your help I may be able to catch this evil person."

"But how can we help? We've already told a policeman all we know."

"I should, however, like to ask a question or two of

my own. You were her best friends and might know something you don't even know you know, if you can understand me. So let's try, shall we?"

They both nodded silently, but Richard could see it was the wife who'd be taking over the talking. Her husband was still too stunned.

"So here we go," he said with his devastatingly charming smile. "I understand Mrs. Clayton came regularly once a week to dinner here. Was it always on a Saturday?"

Mrs. Amberley, as he'd guessed, answered. "It wasn't a fixed engagement. There were several weeks when it wasn't convenient for either one or the other. But, yes, most weeks she came, and it was always on a Saturday."

Jim Findon put a thought into words. "Forgive me for saying so, madam, but why Saturday? I'd have imagined that Sunday's the busiest day of the week for a parson, and you'd want to relax the day before."

For some reason, Mrs. Amberley shot a guilty look at her husband, but she answered. "That's why, because the next day's Sunday. My husband takes his work seriously and agonizes over his sermons. So I try to provide a little distraction on Saturday evening, and nobody was better than Laura at helping him unwind. She could make him laugh, and being the understanding person she was, she always left early. Some people tend to outstay their welcome...not," she added hastily, "that anybody's ever unwelcome, but you see what I mean."

To Richard, the vicar looked slightly startled at this disclosure, and it was plain he'd never suspected his wife of such duplicity on his behalf. He took her hand and squeezed it gently.

"So," Richard shifted to the edge of his chair, "this

Saturday arrangement was well known, I take it?"

"I suppose so, but who'd be interested?" she asked.

He ignored the question and asked another. "Did Mrs. Clayton have evening engagements with other friends?"

The Amberleys' eyes met, searchng for guidance, as if they seemed doubtful what answer to give. Mrs. Amberley was the spokeswoman again. "Not in quite the same way, not what I'd call a private affair like ours was. There were one or two civic functions we all went to; sometimes an engagement party or ruby wedding party or something like that to which we'd go in a crowd. We always gave Laura a lift on those occasions."

Then, curiously, she came up with almost the same words as Milly's. "It's a strange thing in Burshill. Usually there seem to be a preponderance of widows in most places, but not here for some reason. And Laura was conscious of being odd man out, so to speak. Being of an older generation, we still like to have a well-balanced seating arrangement at our tables, and there weren't any unattached men to pair her with. It must sound dreadfully stuffy and old-fashioned to you young men, but that's how we were brought up."

Richard's charming smile was evident again. "I quite understand what you mean. My own mother is horrified at these television dinners they advertise. She couldn't eat if she wasn't sitting at a properly laid table."

Mrs. Amberley smiled back gratefully. "So you see, as far as I know, Laura would go out rarely unless it was to some sort of public function." She added, as an afterthought, "The only couple she ever dined with on her own was the Burys—Sir John and Lady Bury. They were very kind to Laura when she lost her husband, but then

Lady Bury became ill and eventually died, so that was that."

"And the habit wasn't resumed with the second Lady Bury?" Richard asked.

"No, it wasn't!" the vicar's wife replied, with a significant amount of force. "Sir John is quite lost to us now; his second wife is most unsociable."

Then it appeared she hastily recalled her Christian spirit and added, "Poor woman! One shouldn't really blame her. It can't be easy being anyone's second wife, and in her case, made more difficult because Sarah Bury was so popular. She was loved by all, just like poor Laura was, and the present Lady Bury must feel everyone is making comparisons. I would guess she's taking the easy way out by not giving anyone a chance to make those comparisons."

Richard started on another track. "Now, Mrs. Amberely, I want you to think most carefully about my next question. Milly Patcham told me that as well as your dinner engagements, you and Mrs. Clayton met at other times casually."

"Oh, hardly a day went by without, possibly only for a few words. As you know, we live so close. Even with the park between us we can actually see each other's houses quite clearly."

"Right. Now did you notice any significant changes in Mrs. Clayton? Perhaps she was a little worried, puzzled, just something not quite like herself? We'll say, oh, any time during the past six months? Even if you thought it trivial, tell me about it. Take your time."

Mrs. Amberley took him at his word. She considered long and deeply. Then she sighed and shook her head. "I'm sorry, but I can think of nothing I can't account for.

I'll say with all modesty that if she had anything worrying her, she would have told me. But Laura was a completely happy and contented woman. The only grief, and it was bitter, was losing her husband. Apart from that she had a devoted son who'd never been the slightest problem, no money worries, and plenty to occupy her mind."

If Richard was disappointed, he didn't show it; but he thought that was about all he could hope for. Then, to everyone's surprise, the vicar, whom Richard was beginning to think had been struck dumb, opened his mouth and spoke.

"You did say anything trivial, didn't you, Chief Inspector?"

"Yes, vicar, anything, however small."

Hesitantly, the good man contributed his mite of information. "My dear wife was poorly over Christmas, very poorly indeed, so I forbade her to go to Midnight Mass on Christmas Eve. Yes," he said, wondering at himself, "I put my foot down. Laura had been most kind, but her family was with her for the holiday, so I wouldn't have been surprised if she hadn't attended, either. But she came alone as the baby couldn't be left."

The Vicar pulled at his shirt as if adjusting his robe. "When the service was over, I told her I would see her home. I took off my robe, and she was sitting in her pew waiting for me. I was a little surprised by the look on her face, as if she was miles away. I thought," he said humbly, "she might have been caught up in the magical spirit of the moment, but I fear it wasn't. I spoke to her, but she didn't answer. Then she shook herself out of whatever dream she was in and said, 'Funny!'"

Shaking his head also, he carried on. "I didn't ask her what she meant and we walked together to her house. My wife is right, you know, Laura was always excellent at helping me relax, and usually had a little joke at my expense, though kindly, I do assure you. But on this night she was very quiet, not like herself at all, and when we arrived at her home I ventured to ask if anything was wrong."

He stopped, casting his mind back, striving to remember the exact words. "She laughed and said, 'No, nothing wrong, George. I had a bit of a shock tonight. Thought I saw someone I knew a long time ago, but it couldn't have been.' And that was all. Just a silly little thing, but I thought I'd mention it."

Chapter Fifteen

Sergeant Findon looked as if he was about to giggle. Richard was reminded of a game they played at his nursery school, something about 'When father says stand, we all stand!' It was a bit like that when he went into one of his trances. Everybody maintained a respectful silence, waiting for the Oracle to speak.

But he wasn't in a trance. His brain was ticking over working out a mental timetable. Yes, it all fit. Laura saw Marie for the first time on Christmas Eve, decided she was imagining things, or realized she was mistaken. Wrote to her friend, Rosemary Marden, in South Africa to tell her about it, and on the last day of March, she was killed. Three months in all, just over. There were matters here to be thought over later.

His eyes focused again on his silent audience.

Mrs. Amberely was the first to utter. "You didn't say anything to me, George, about that incident."

"I didn't think it was worth mentioning, my dear, and I'm sure it's of no consequence to the Chief Inspector, either."

"On the contrary, vicar. I think you've just told me something of considerable importance."

George appeared puzzled but gratified.

"I suppose it'd be impossible for you to remember who was at church that night?"

The vicar smiled, rather sadly. "I'm afraid my usual congregations are so sparse I could put a name to everyone in it. But for just a few occasions during the year, the turnout is bigger, and the Midnight Mass is one of them. I don't recollect any outstanding strangers, though."

"Let's try and reach it another way. Where did Mrs. Clayton sit?"

"In her usual place, the third pew from the front."

"So she'd have a limited view, wouldn't she? I don't imagine she was the kind of lady to turn around and stare, was she?"

"Indeed not!" The vicar was horrified, but he was beginning to catch on, and even becoming interested. "Let me think. Those of my parishioners who only turn out on Remembrance Day, Easter, or Christmas tend to sit well back in the church. Strange how old customs linger. It was always the notables who sat in front, and the lesser fry at the back. Not that the notables round about are always good churchgoers, I'm afraid."

"Then Mrs. Clayton would have seen anyone in the three front pews on either side of the aisle; is that a fair assessment, sir?"

"I think so, yes. And now you'll be asking if I can remember who was there in front of me. Oh dear!"

Mrs. Amberley joined in. "I know I wasn't there on that particular night, but I can give you a hint, George, as to who usually marches up to the front to be sure of being recognized!"

"Julia!" he expostulated. "That's a most unkind thing to say!"

"But true!" his unrepentant wife said. "I'm not such a saint as my husband, Chief Inspector, and I know a lot of the locals come to church to make a good impression. If they gain any spiritual comfort from it, that's a bonus. Now, George, I'll say some names, and you try to remember if they were there last Christmas and where they were sitting."

The poor man looked quite shattered but nodded his head. Mrs. Amberley closed her eyes and reeled off a list of names, adding their professional or business titles for Richard's benefit.

The list was long and comprehensive, including tradespeople, doctors, bank managers, teachers at local schools, Sir John and Lady Bury, and presidents of various organizations.

Jim scribbled furiously until she ran out of steam. Then the vicar agreed that most of those she'd mentioned were certainly there last Christmas; he'd shaken hands with them at the church door after the service.

"Add up the total," Richard told Jim and when it was done, asked the vicar if the amount tallied with the space available.

"More than enough to fill those three pews, well, six, counting both sides of the aisle. And, really, Inspector, all the people my wife mentioned would have been known to poor Laura anyway. I honestly can't remember any strangers, not even when I stood at the door afterwards. It isn't everyone who stops to say goodnight; many slip away without a word."

At Richard's request, the vicar took the two policemen into the church, Mrs. Amberley tagging along. He asked to be shown where Laura usually sat and seated himself in the same place.

Richard asked the vicar to stand in the pulpit, while Jim and Mrs. Amberley carried out various orders. He had them walking down the aisle behind him; sitting in different parts; popping up and down like yoyos; while he watched them from various angles of his head.

"Where did Sir John and Lady Bury sit?" he called up to the vicar—a question which made Jim look at him curiously.

The Chief Constable and his wife had their own positions for years, he was told; they were in the front row of Laura's block. Jim had to sit there also.

Richard was going to great lengths to get an accurate picture with this church episode. "And looking down on us, you still can't recall any strangers in these six sets of pews?"

The poor vicar cast his eyes downward and then up to the roof as if seeking heavenly guidance but had to confess he could recollect nothing useful. In the end, they left—Richard putting a handsome donation into the Poor Box, for which the vicar thanked him gratefully.

"Seems as if that's where the fuse was lit, doesn't it, sir?" Jim said as they drove back to the Station. "But why did the murderer wait from Christmas till April before acting?"

"That's a point that's puzzling me," Richard said. "But if Mrs. Clayton decided she'd made a mistake on the first occasion, the murderer may have done the same, thought it was imagination, if she even noticed Laura, that is. Somewhere between Christmas Eve and the 31st of March, they must have met again and realized they were right in the first place. I'd give a good deal to know where and when. What's so bloody aggravating," he mused, half to himself, "is that I think the vicar could supply me with a lot of information I want."

"Why didn't you ask him then?" a justifiably puzzled Jim enquired.

"Because I'm treading on the most delicate of eggshells at the moment. I'm waiting for the result of another enquiry I've put in motion, and if I don't get an answer soon, I'll have to begin smashing some of those eggshells!"

* * * *

At home, Richard got on with routine work and knocked off about seven o'clock. Shortly after dinner, the phone rang and it was Geoffrey Brede.

"Wotcher, Richard!" he said amiably.

"And you! How's crime?"

"Keeping me off the dole queue. You busy with your chicken rustlers and knicker-nappers?"

"Reasonably so." Richard answered.

"So you wouldn't be missed if you took a day off and came to the big city?"

"Don't suppose so. When do you suggest?"

"How about tomorrow? I'll show you the Houses of Parliament and give you lunch."

"Good idea. I think I'll bring my mother along for the ride. Any chance of your good lady being free to take her window-shopping?"

"Easily arranged, old lad. See you in the morning sometime then."

"Sure thing. Tell you what, I'll bring one of my sergeants along, too—give him a treat."

"Suit yourself. All will be welcome."

They rang off, and Richard stood by the phone for a long moment. Kate would have definitely compared him to the devil at that moment. He and Geoffrey knew each other's code well enough. Geoff wanted him in London urgently.

He rang Sergeant Findon.

"Any plans for tonight, Jim?"

Jim gave an exaggerated groan. "I don't think it

matters, does it, sir?"

"Not really. Will you pack a toothbrush, clean shirt, and socks, and be here about tennish? We'll talk tonight, and tomorrow I'm taking you walkies to London, actually. You'd better stop the night because I've a feeling it'll turn into a late night sitting. okay?"

"Very much okay, sir," said a jubilant Jim. "Shall I phone the Station and tell them where we'll be?"

"No, we'll leave it until the morning. See you later."

"Now what are you up to?" Ella asked exasperatedly.

"If you're a good girl, I'm taking you to London tomorrow. Jim's coming too, as you heard."

"It's to do with the case, isn't it?"

"Anyone would think we only had the one case going," Richard grumbled. "But I know which one you mean. The answer's yes, and that's your lot for now."

After one nightcap with Jim who'd arrived promptly as instructed and dressed in his finest, Ella took herself off to bed.

"Good God! You look like a stockbroker," was Richard's comment. "Hope I shan't show you up!"

They sat. "I'll let you have one more drink, a small one. You need a clear head for what I'm going to tell you."

"Better put the bottle away, sir," Jim suggested. "To keep us out of temptation."

"No," Richard said, with a straight face. "I'll want to wet my whistle occasionally. I expect to be hoarse by the time this lot's out."

The preliminaries were over. Jim had now heard of Richard's activities in America and France. He had listened to Cassy's tape. Richard withheld nothing from Jim, except his own theories. Jim looked like he was hovering between the states of astonishment and disbelief for more than two hours. Richard really was hoarse by the end of the recital.

"My God!" Jim, said, almost in awe. "What a fantastic story! This will add to your reputation!"

Richard suddenly felt terribly weary; he sagged back against the chair, eyes closed. "I've had incredible luck," he said. "No genius was necessary to follow the leads I was given. One thing led to another automatically."

Richard could see that Jim was probably thinking his comment was unduly modest. Especially as Jim would expect Richard to have more up his sleeve.

"Do you think our visit to London will finish the job, sir? And if it's not too rude a question, why do you want me along? Shall we be making an arrest?"

Richard took his time answering. "No, we shan't be making an arrest tomorrow, but I expect the last piece to slot into the jigsaw. I think I know what its going to be, but I'm saying nothing more now. The reason I'm taking you..." He opened his eyes and gazed steadily at the young Sergeant. "I need a witness to what I shall be saying. If my theories are correct, I may say and do some rather strange things, and I want one of my own lot present to watch and listen. Sorry to sound mysterious, but that's your ration for tonight."

* * * *

All three of them traveled by train; Ella read her book, the two men their newspapers.

After a long train ride to London, the taxi ride from Victoria to New Scotland Yard didn't take long, and Geoffrey Brede, along with his wife, Andrea, was waiting in his office.

Andrea and Ella were old friends and after the introductions to Jim. The two ladies were quickly ready to leave, with instructions to phone about four o'clock.

"And don't forget, Mother," Richard warned Ella, "You're not on expenses. Stick to Woolworth's and keep out of Harrod's!"

As soon as the door closed, the smiles on the men's faces were wiped out. They sat down, Jim on the edge of his chair with interest.

"All right, Geoff. No beating about the bush. You've traced the Westfield girl, I take it?"

"Yes," Geoffrey answered soberly, "and I think you know who it is."

"The second Lady Bury," said Richard with no hesitation.

"Got it in one!" Geoff confirmed.

* * * *

Richard felt no sense of elation or triumph, only a deep sadness for Sir John. Poor Jim was the one who looked like he was stunned with shock and horror.

"Lady Bury!" he blurted out. "And you knew, sir?"

"I haven't known for long, and even at that, I wasn't one hundred per cent sure. That's why I've had to be so careful."

Geoffrey Brede went to a cabinet and produced a bottle and glasses, but Richard waved them away.

"Too much to be done now, thanks. You'll have gathered, I suppose, that our triple murderess—no, four times, more for all I know—is the wife of my Chief Constable. If you think I'm tackling that on my own, think again, my friend."

"For God's sake, tell me about it, then. You've just been throwing your orders for me to carry out, bloody cheek, and not told me a thing."

Richard shook his head. "There are more twists and

turns in this story than there are in Hampton Court maze. It took me a solid couple of hours last night to fill Jim in. I'm not doing it for you and then later on for somebody else. No, this is a job for a higher authority than ours. I know precisely how I want it done, too. So who do you recommend we go and talk to in this rabbit warren? He's got to be a big wheel, mind!"

Geoffrey burst out laughing and turned to Jim. "Is he always like this? Look, I appreciate your problem, and I'll get an appointment to see the right man. But, for God's sake, don't try and tell him how to do his job! He'll throw a tantrum, and believe me, they're spectacular when he does."

"Oh I think he'll see it my way," Richard answered with infuriating calm. Jim looked as if he was praying silently to all the gods he could think of that he would be allowed to be present at the interview.

Geoffrey laughed again. "Oh, go to the devil in your own way. I shall pretend I don't know you very well. Now, it'll take me a while to set this up. Will you go for a walk or wait here and help yourselves to a drink? I've got some mouthwash in the same cabinet."

"We'll wait here," Richard decided. He wasn't feeling quite so calm as he appeared. When Geoffrey left his office, Richard investigated the drink's cupboard.

"Yes, it's okay. There's a gargle here, so I think we'll fortify ourselves with one drink apiece, ready for the Lord High Muck-a-Muck. You look as if you could do with it, Jim."

"I can that!" Jim agreed fervently. "I know you want to save your story for the Big Man, whoever he is, but can't you just tell me when and why you suspected Lady Bury? I shall bust a gut if I have to wait much longer."

"Ah well," Richard said, pouring fairly generous measures of Scotch, "I might as well rehearse on you, I suppose. To begin with, it was sheer prejudice against the woman herself, just as Pierre and Marie felt for her when she was young. The first time I spoke to her, the idle thought crossed my mind that she resembled Lady Macbeth and how suitable it would be if we could pin the murders on her."

With a smile on his face, he looked at Jim saying, "I laughed at myself at the time, but couldn't help thinking also, that she was in as good a position as anyone to know everything we were doing. There were two other points. She was supposed to be away from home the night Mrs. Clayton was killed, and she was in London, supposedly for the Ballet, when Mrs. Marden got the chop. Another point in my thinking was about the jobs being done by an expert in anatomy. I wondered about doctors, nurses, and such like people. Lady Bury had a habit of shooting her cuffs and tugging her belt that suggested she was used to being in uniform of some kind."

He sipped his drink; continued.

"These were only idle speculations as I said, but I thought about the lady quite a bit, and when I heard Pierre and Marie describing her as a girl, the phrases they used were almost identical with those I'd applied to Lady Bury. Their talk about her being a nurse when she left school seemed to tally as well. But, of course, outwardly it all seemed a load of codswallop." Richard shook his head and carried on with the story.

"Then a remark from the French Marie, something about an idea she had that the Westfield girl was distantly related to one of the six, gave me an idea of my own. When I got back home, I phoned Mrs. Kanderhagen.

in California and asked her if she could remember whether any of her lot had a relation who was in line for the school. She said she seemed to recollect Sarah Brenchley talking about a second cousin or someone who wanted to attend. She was definitely certain it was Sarah, because Sarah, normally such a nice girl, had added that she hoped it wouldn't be in her time because she couldn't stand the girl and would never speak to her if she could help it whenever they met."

He sipped again, sighed, and went on. "So you see it didn't take a lot of hard work on my part. Intuition, coincidence, luck. But I hope you realize what it all amounts to."

"No hard evidence, sir," Jim said promptly.

"Good man. No, we've no evidence. That's why I've hatched my latest plot, and if I can get the gent to agree here, we've nailed her."

"Will I be allowed to sit in, sir?" Jim asked eagerly.

"You will indeed. The hardest part's yet to come, and I want you as witness. Now drink up and then we'll gargle and hope we don't have to wait much longer."

It seemed an eternity before Geoffrey returned, and when he did, he was rather subdued. "Well, God help you. I've done better, or worse, than I thought. One of the real High-ups was in my chap's office decided he'd like to sit in. He's another peppery old cuss but as clever as all-get-out, so watch your step and make out a good case or your career's down the drain! Ready?"

"Thanks for the tip." Richard smiled. "Doesn't look as if I'll get your vote of confidence. But just watch. I'll come out smelling of roses."

He rather wished he felt more confident himself, but there was no turning back. He and Geoff, with Jim close on their heels, went to the office pointed out, entered, saluted smartly, and were invited to sit.

Three hours later, they were let off the leash to eat, with strict instructions to be back in ninety minutes. Richard had put his case with clarity and precision; the tape had been played; all in what could have been an unnerving silence had he not been so engrossed in what he was saying.

When he'd come to the end, he waited for the questions. They were fired at him from two angles, one after the other. He refused to let himself be hurried, and if an answer required thought, he sat until he'd got the right one. On the whole, he felt he'd done fairly well, but the real tussle would come after lunch. By mutual agreement, the three of them went out to a restaurant instead of eating in the building, and also by mutual agreement, they kept off the subject uppermost in their minds.

Back they went when time was up. Richard had his plan of campaign mapped out now, having taken the measure of the two V.I.P. policemen and went straight into the attack without waiting for the courtesies. He told them exactly how he would like the matter dealt with, also why and when. To everyone's surprise but his own, and possibly Jim's, he won his battle without a shot fired in anger.

As he told Geoff afterwards, "I think they were so stymied, they were glad of my suggestions."

"Suggestions be buggered!" Geoff said. "You sat there and told them what to do! I never thought I'd live to see the day when those two would cave in meekly. They like the orders to come from on high, not from a tuppeny-ha'penny Detective Chief Inspector."

Richard laughed. "Yes, but let's be reasonable about

it. What else can we do? Wait for that bloody maniac woman to do somebody else in?"

Before that conversation, there were many things to be discussed with the lords of Scotland Yard; plans to be put into operation immediately; and a watertight timetable to be drawn up for subsequent movements. Suggestions were made by each of them, including Jim. Some were discarded, some kept, until eventually they had a workable scheme afoot.

Richard was congratulated—he couldn't quite think what for as the affair was going to be highly embarrassing. The Press would have a field day. But he'd got what he wanted, and if anything went wrong he'd be the one to carry the can. That was made plain, along with the congratulations.

From then on, every event was as planned and rehearsed, every possible contingency thought about, as a military maneuver. The first snag cropped up about ten minutes after they left the Presence, but if nothing worse happened, they'd no need to worry. As the first step, Geoffrey was to go home, pack a bag, and return with the Hayward party.

"Oh Lord!" Richard said. "That's dicey. I've only got two bedrooms furnished as yet."

"Do you think your mother would like to sleep with me, sir?" Jim queried.

That broke his two ribald superiors right up; their comments would stay in his memory a long time. But the tension was snapped, and it was a fairly happy lot who returned home ready for the next operation. The problem of Ella was solved after Geoff had a quiet word with his wife.

"Mrs. Hayward, would you do me a great big favour?

Come and stay with me while Geoff's away. I hate being on my own. I can lend you whatever you need for a day or so, or we could run down in the morning and pick up some of your own."

Ella looked doubtfully at Richard who nodded to her. He suspected that his mother wasn't too pleased at being bundled out of the way, and he didn't suppose Andrea was exactly thrilled at having an unwanted guest shoved on her, either.

However, it was settled upon. Geoffrey commandeered a vehicle from the car pool; they all went back to his house in Chelsea where he flung a few oddments into a bag then the women were left behind, and the men went back to Burshill in Geoffrey's own car.

"Prefer to have my own transport," he explained. The Detective Sergeant who usually worked with him would be down on the train in the morning.

"Now you can have him to sleep with." Jim was informed with amusement.

"If it's all the same to you, sir, I'd rather have your mother!" was Jim's spirited retort. Back in Burshill, he was sent on his way with a long list of instructions from the other two, including, "Don't get tight and shoot your mouth off." And "Don't go taking to any strange women!"

Richard's eyes followed Findon's retreating back, a half smile on his face. "Poor Findon!" he said. "It's going to be difficult for him to settle down again when this is all over. I hope he won't expect a constant diet of murders and gallivanting to London."

"I shouldn't worry," his friend told him dryly. "Things seem to happen wherever you go. Burshill will probably have the highest crime rate in the country before you've been here a year!"

"Shut your face, and come and look at my funny little house. Tell me if you think my Kate will like what we've done."

Chapter Sixteen

"Well I'm impressed," Geoffrey Brede told Richard. "Burshill Police Station is clean, bright, airy, and modern, and only completed two years back."

"I've seen the old Station," Richard told him. "Straight out of Dickens, I kid you not! Wouldn't have suited me at all. The town's expanding at such a rate, they needed this."

The Yard man was introduced, but the purpose of his visit was left obscure.

The plan began to work halfway through the morning. Sir John phoned.

"Good morning, Hayward. I've just had a call from a chap at Scotland Yard, tells me they're sending a fellow down for a few days. Know anything about it?"

"Yes, I do, sir. In fact he's here already, came last night. I knew about it but couldn't contact you as you were away at a conference."

"What's he doing with us?"

"We're cooperating over these linked murders, Sir John. He'll be looking into our files, talking to various people—you know the sort of thing," vaguely. "A Sergeant will be coming today."

"Hm!" Sir John answered. "Well, see he's taken care off, won't you? Give him everything he wants. Where's he staying?"

"With me, sir. As luck would have it, we're well known to each other from the old days, so I'm putting him up."

"Good, good. Let me know if anything transpires. How is your mother?"

"Very well, thank you. She's away at the moment, staying with friends. And Lady Bury? Is she well?"

"Couldn't be better, buzzing about, here, there, and everywhere."

When he rang off, Richard gave Geoffrey the conversation, adding, "Now where's she 'buzzing about' to? Thought she never went anywhere." He seemed faintly worried.

"Can't do much about it at the moment, so stop flapping. When my chap gets here, he and Findon can sort out the observation details. Then we wait."

"Wonder what she'll make of this when she hears the news."

"Hope it rattles her good and plenty!"

"Don't be too sure of that, Geoff. I've met the lady. I don't think she'll scare too easily."

* * * *

Detective Sergeant Heath was met by Findon, and the four men went into a huddle. Heath was older than Jim, but they hit it off from the start. When they'd finished talking, the two Sergeants left with instructions to report to Richard at his home sometime during the evening. But Jim arrived at teatime, slightly perturbed.

"Thought you ought to know at once, sir. The lady went to Brightport and visited Thomas Cook's. Heath wandered in after her, and she came out with a stack of travel brochures."

"Where to?" Richard asked sharply.

"All sorts of places, nowhere in particular. Do you think she's getting ready to skip?"

Both Richard and Geoffrey became silent, each with

their own thoughts. Coming out of his dream like state, Richard answered Jim.

"Not just yet, I wouldn't think. Could be quite an innocent thing, sorting out their holiday or something. Or maybe she's preparing to do a bunk if she suspects we're getting warm. But she won't run off empty-handed, I'll bet on that. No. I reckon we've got a day or two, and that's all we need."

Nothing of any consequence occurred on the following day except that Sir John phoned again to ask how Mr. Brede was getting on.

"I would come in and see him personally, but my wife's a bit under the weather at the moment. Serves me right for saying she couldn't be better, doesn't it?"

"Nothing serious, I hope," Richard said courteously.

"Oh no. She may be coming down with a cold, but you know what women are. She likes me to be with her."

"Poor old devil!" Geoffrey said when the short call was over. "What the hell's he going to do when this breaks?"

"God knows!" Richard answered. "He'll have to resign, of course. I only hope his friends rally round to help. It's going to hit the whole place hard—well, the older residents at least."

They let another day go by in which nothing much happened. The lady, it was reported, hadn't moved out of the house, but she and Sir John had been seen walking round the garden. In the evening, a lengthy call was made by Richard to Scotland Yard.

"Easter next week," Geoffrey said to Richard. "Hope I get my hot cross buns in my own house!"

"You will!" Richard was definite. "Tomorrow we move."

Early in the morning, a brief call from the 'higher uppers' in Scotland Yard, London, started the ball rolling.

"All set!" Richard said. "We'll give it half an hour and be on our way. You all know what you've got to do?"

His three helpers nodded as none of them felt like talking, it seemed.

Richard drove alone to Sir John's house, the others a discreet distance behind. He asked the cleaning woman who answered his knock on the door if he could speak with Sir John, and without waiting for permission, the good lady showed him straight into the drawing room.

Lady Bury was sitting there talking to her husband, and both seemed startled at his sudden appearance. Sir John stood up and came forward. To Richard's compassionate eyes, he appeared older and grey in the face. This affair had taken its toll.

"This is a surprise, Hayward," Sir John said, "I wasn't expecting you."

"I'm sorry about that, sir," Richard replied, nodding gravely to Lady Bury. He only glanced at her. She seemed much the same as when he'd been in this room before. "But I have something to say."

Sir John checked the time on his watch.

"It'll have to be a quick word, I'm afraid. I've been called to an urgent meeting at Scotland Yard. Have to be leaving soon."

"I'll see you aren't late for your train, Sir John. I think I know what they want to talk to you about at the Yard."

The Chief Constable looked slightly affronted as it wasn't etiquette for an underling to know something before he did!

"The fact is, sir," Richard went on, "I want to be taken off the Clayton case."

Sir John was startled; Lady Bury gave an unpleasant laugh and said in a mocking voice, "Dear me, Inspector! And I was told what a clever young man you are. Proving too much for you, is it?"

Richard ignored her. Sir John, with a return to his old authoritative way, said, "Please keep quiet, my dear. Now, Hayward, what's this all about? Why do you want to be taken off the Clayton murder?"

"I've had a long talk to my friend, Detective Chief Inspector Brede, and we've decided it'll be better for the Yard to take over all three cases. They've already been asked to tackle the Heathrow murder, also the murder of Miss Sidley. They have all the facilities we haven't and will treat the three as having been done by the same person."

Again Lady Bury intervened in spite of a majestic frown from her husband. "I thought it was decided that Mrs. Clayton's murder was coincidence."

Richard's head rotated sharply toward her, and he replied coldly, "You may have thought that, but Scotland Yard thinks otherwise. There are too many things which definitely link all three women together."

He turned back to Sir John. "In a way, it's an admission of defeat on my part, but there will be quite a good liaison between us and the Yard people. I have several interesting points to contribute with what I learned in America and France."

He didn't dare to look at Lady Bury, but from the corner of his eye, he saw a slight involuntary movement.

"France!" Sir John echoed in surprise. "I didn't know you'd been to France. When was that?"

"I haven't had a chance to see you or indeed to have told you I was going," Richard evaded. "As I said yesterday, you were in the North. Anyhow, I knew you'd have no objection. You want this mess cleared up as much as anyone."

"That's true," Sir John sighed. "I don't feel as if I can rest until poor Laura's death is avenged. Well, if this is what you want and it's what the Yard's going to talk to me about, I'll agree."

Lady Bury broke in again. "Surely there's no need for you to go off to London now, John. If that's all they're going to talk about, it can be settled over the phone."

Richard held his breath, but Sir John drew himself up. "Of course I shall go. It's only right that I should discuss it thoroughly with those in authority." Looking at his watch, he said, "And it's time I was off. You know I like to be at the station in good time." He picked up his briefcase, searched around to see he had everything, and prepared to leave.

Lady Bury made one last effort. "You could always plead illness, and it wouldn't be a lie. You've not been feeling well since this miserable business started."

He took no notice, walked into the hall, and picked up his hat. He said goodbye to his wife and stood aside to let Richard leave first.

This was Richard's opportunity. Turning to Lady Bury to make his farewells, he looked her full in the face, and said, "I'm sure Sir John will learn a great deal from his trip to London, and when he gets back, with your previous nursing experience, Lady Bury, you should know what to do for him."

His gaze locked with hers, and it would have been hard to determine whose eyes were the hardest and coldest. Without another word, he walked out, Sir John following. The door closed behind them.

Richard waited until Sir John's car left the drive then got into his own car and pulled away. Out of sight of the house he stopped, backed, and waited. The second vehicle came up behind him and parked; he went up to it and got in beside Geoffrey.

"Well, how did it go?" was the eager question.

Richard related the entire conversation.

"Did she get the message?" Geoffrey asked.

"Loud and clear. She's no fool, and I'm certain she knows that I know. The question now is, will she have sense enough to realize we've no proof. If she chooses to sit tight, we'll be hamstrung, but I'm banking on the hope that she won't realize that and do something daft for the first time."

Jim spoke up unexpectedly. "She'll be doing us all a favour if she shoots her bloody self!"

There was a general laugh.

"I agree," Richard said, "but that woman's sense of self-preservation is strong. Right; I'm off back again on my tod. I'll be just out of sight of the house round the curve in the drive. The rest of you take up the agreed positions and pray it doesn't rain. We might be in for a long wait."

"Do you think we ought to cut the telephone wires?" Jim asked helpfully. "If she's in the house too long, isn't there a possibility Sir John will ring?"

Richard cuffed him around the ears gently. "You watch too much telly, Jim! It'll be a couple of hours before he gets to the Yard, and there he'll get the run-around until we ring."

"Oh, God!" Geoffrey groaned. "I hope to hell your plans work. We'll all be put out to grass if they don't."

"Have no fear, children. I saw the look in the lady's

eyes. You didn't! Something diabolical's going to happen. I only wish I knew what!"

With that he left, and the others took up their appointed places. Richard left his car before the last bend to the house and stood amongst the trees and bushes which were dense enough to give coverage but with enough peepholes for him to see the front door.

Heath would be at the back, although it was an unlikely exit; there were miles of fields leading only to the Downs. The wait seemed endless.

It was, in fact, an hour and a half before the action began. Everything happened then with almost the speed of light. The front door opened, and Lady Bury stepped out. She was wearing a mink coat—far too hot for the beautiful Spring day—and carried two heavily weighted down suitcases. A large shoulder bag hung over her arm. *As I thought*, Richard said to himself, *she's not going empty-handed.*

She started towards the two-car garage, and while her back was to him, he ran up behind her in crepe-soled shoes and addressed her pleasantly. "Going on holiday, Lady Bury? To Leveisin, perhaps?"

She moved so quickly he was nearly caught unawares. It was quite horrifying; she disintegrated in front of him; the suave, sophisticated woman turned into an animal. She didn't scream, but a low sound issued from her throat, almost like a growl, and quick as a flash, she dropped the cases and from her pocket he saw the gleam of something long and thin and wicked.

The thrust went straight for his heart, and so fast and strong and accurate was her aim, it actually penetrated the thick padding he was wearing and drew a gout of blood. He grabbed her arm, twisted it to make her drop the surgical instrument, which, indeed, it was, and as Geoffrey and Jim ran up, he began his set piece.

"Lady Bury, I arrest you for the murder of Laura Clayton on Saturday, March 31..."

* * * *

"But I still don't quite understand why you had to go in for all that cloak and dagger stuff. Why the elaborate charade? If you were so certain she was guilty, why didn't you just arrest her?" Ella asked.

"Because we had no proof," Richard explained patiently. "We had a tricky situation on our plate. She was wife to the Chief Constable, for God's sake! The whole idea was to make her crack by degrees, and thank the Lord it worked. She guessed I was on to her, and she wasn't going to wait until I spilled the whole can of beans. She thought, you see, the Yard people had only just become involved. Actually, I think she went a bit doolally and wasn't working it out logically."

Geoffrey said, "I still break out into a cold sweat every now and again, thinking of a hundred and one things that could have gone wrong."

The conversation was taking place in the evening of the day after the arrest. It had been a grueling time for all concerned, during which Richard had snatched a few minutes to give Ella a list of phone calls he wanted her to make—to Alec Clayton, the Kanderhagens, Harry in California, and Pierre in France. All she had to tell them was that the case was over, and he'd be in touch with details when he was free.

The four policemen had spent a long time with the Almighty Ones at Scotland Yard, and when the interview ended, Richard had been asked to stop on for a minute.

The high-ranking officer present addressed him

severely. "I've congratulated you publicly on the outcome of this affair, but now I'm giving you a private warning. I've heard of your unconventional methods and, personally, I feel at times you're unorthodox to the point of insubordination. This is tolerated because you get results, but if you ever lose a case through some bloody stupid whim of your own, you'll be for the high-jump. Understood?"

"Understood, sir." Richard said gravely. Outside the door, he grinned. It wasn't the first time he'd been addressed with much the same words, and he doubted if it would be the last.

Sergeant Heath was absent, but he'd taken Findon with him to Chelsea to fetch Ella home. She and Andrea wanted to know what and how it had happened, so he and Geoffrey were bringing them up to date.

"And has she confessed?" Ella asked.

"Singing like a bird," Richard said. "She seems to be obsessed with her own cleverness and only too happy to let everyone know how brilliant she is. No remorse at all."

"Do you think a lawyer will plead insanity?" Geoffrey asked.

"God knows!" Richard was beginning to feel overly tired. "I'd have thought any woman who could commit such appalling acts must be mad, but I think she's sane enough to get a life sentence. Where they'll put her, I don't know, but as long as it's out of my way, I don't much care, either. It'll be a while before the trial comes on. There's such a mass of evidence now, and witnesses to be called from all over the place. Perhaps she'll have time to think and deny the lot. She's potty enough."

"I've got to ask, although I don't think I can bear to hear the answer," Ella said, "but how did Sir John take it?"

Geoffrey and Richard looked at each other. Richard took it on himself to give the reply.

"Quietly, I gather. He told them he'd met her in Canada—that's where she went after the war—when he stopped off on his trip round the world. She was very sympathetic about his loss—a charming woman, he thought her, poor devil. She spun him some tale about being much in the same boat herself except she'd been left a penniless widow. We've got to go into all that previous history, of course. Anyway, the upshot was that somehow or other she got him to propose. He seemed a bit hazy on that, and my guess is that she made all the running, and he didn't realize what he'd let himself in for."

"Did he know she was a relation of his first wife?"

"He says not, but I'm sure she knew. It would appeal to her warped sense of humour to think she was getting all the things Sarah had once possessed."

"Poor man," Ella said gently. "I pity him so much. How can he bear to live with the knowledge that his own wife killed the lady he was so fond of? It would be enough to destroy him."

"You needn't pity him, Mother," Richard said quietly. "He died this morning."

Ella was aghast. "Oh Richard! Not suicide?"

"No. Heart attack. I thought he seemed ill and grey when I saw him at the house. Apparently he'd had a dicky heart for some while, and this finished him off. I'm truly glad he didn't commit suicide. I liked the old boy. Well, he's out of it, thank God."

They were quiet for a few minutes, thinking of that unhappy man. Fuzz, right on cue, created a diversion by bringing out the remains of Geoff's slipper and presenting it to him proudly, as some kind of trophy.

The tension broken as Geoffrey delivered himself of some well chosen remarks which Fuzz interpreted as compliments, wagging his wispy tail in appreciation. Geoffrey gave up in despair and poured drinks all round.

Richard recovered his spirits a little. "Only a small one for Jim," he said. "He's got to drive us home in a minute."

"If I work much more with you, sir," Jim said reproachfully, "I shall find myself becoming a celibate tee-totaller!"

Richard eyed him appraisingly. "Then you'd better sign the pledge and buy yourself a single bed. I like the way you've handled yourself over this case. We'll be working together many times, I hope."

Jim went pink with pleasure.

"There are still lots of things I want to know," Ella began again. "It's obvious now how Lady Bury got all her information so quickly and could act on it, but if you're right, Richard, why didn't she and Mrs. Clayton meet until Christmas Eve? I thought Alec's mother and Sir John were such great friends. Wouldn't she have been one of the first to meet his new wife?"

"Good point, but a simple explanation. Nobody who mentioned Sir John's remarriage said exactly when he was married again. I put a few tactful questions to the vicar's wife later on, after the Christmas Eves' business came to light. He didn't bring the new Lady Bury home until September, and by a series of the most extraordinary flukes, Laura was about the only one of his friends who didn't meet the woman."

Taking a sip of his drink, Richard went on. "She was on holiday herself when he came back which accounted for three weeks or so. She'd only been home herself a few days when young Alec's wife was on the last knockings with the expected baby, so up she went to look after her, staying on for a while when the baby was born. Then it seems Sir John and his wife were away off and on at various conferences. He was a conscientious soul where his various activities were concerned, and so it went on. He and Laura telephoned each other occasionally, but from what everyone told me about her, she was an unassuming lady who would never dream of turning up on a person's doorstep without an invitation. Maybe she thought the newlyweds wanted to be alone."

"At their age!" a scandalized Jim interrupted, earning himself a frown from Ella.

"We're not quite past it at that age!" she told him. He looked totally disbelieving.

"Anyway," Richard resumed, "you can take it from me the two women didn't clap eyes on each other until Sir John dragged his lady to Midnight Mass. Laura was shaken but obviously put it down to a chance likeness."

Richard shrugged his shoulders. "My guess is that the Bury woman found out from Sir John who Laura was and may have started making her plans at that stage. From what she's been spilling out to the Yard boys, they met head-on...wait for it...at the annual Police Ball of all things. Sir John would have thought it his duty to go. What was said, we don't know, nor shall we ever know what Laura said in her letter to Mrs. Marden. There are a lot of things we can only guess at, but they aren't too important. Not important enough to jeopardize our case, but I'm bound to confess I'd love to know out of sheer curiosity."

"Did she confess to killing that French maid?" Ella asked next.

"She did, but they haven't discovered so far what the other girls knew about it or what she thought they knew. In fact, what really started her off on her orgy of murders. There's no doubt, Mother, you were right when you said our then unknown X was trying to preserve her reputation. I doubt whether, at this late date, anything could have been proved against her about the original murder, but it wouldn't have suited her to have even a whisper of gossip. After a lifetime of being one of the have-nots—and I bet she kept that chip on her shoulder all through like the French Marie said she had—she was now a Somebody. Lady Bury, no less, and nothing or nobody would be allowed to stand in her way."

"What a dreadful, awful woman," Ella shuddered. "But I can see now what you meant about having no proof. You had to do something drastic to flush her out. Thank God she didn't attack you!"

Richard winked at Geoffrey. There were one or two little matters best kept from the ladies' tender ears.

"But what about—?"

"Oh, Mother, for pity's sake give it a rest now, will you? I'll answer all your other questions tomorrow, if I can, that is. There is still a hell of a lot of things we've still got to ferret out ourselves. Let's go home, please."

Ella told Richard that he sounded like the little boy he once was, tired and cross after a long day at the seaside. She stood up and began to collect her belongings. Fuzz trotted out with his own luggage—Geoff's other slipper.

"I wonder if I could claim for a new pair on my expense's sheet?" a resigned Geoffrey asked.

Amidst the small flurry of preparations for departure, they suddenly realized the telephone bell was ringing.

Geoffrey answered it.

"Oh, good evening, sir," he said, raising his eyebrows comically at Richard who stood to attention and saluted in an exaggerated manner. "Yes, he's here. Just leaving, actually."

The voice at the other end quacked steadily away; Geoffrey's face became quite expressionless. After the speech finished, he said, "Thank you, sir. Yes, I'll tell him."

He replaced the receiver with care. "Well, none of your further questions will be answered. The lady's done herself in."

"What!" came a concerted exclamation.

"Poisoned herself! God knows where she had it hidden. She was searched, of course, but it was somewhere. She's dead, so that's really the end of the case, Richard."

Epilogue

His instructions were clear to his mother. Ella wasn't to wake him up for any reason at all, not even if the house was on fire! He'd sleep the clock round if he felt like it.

So Richard wasn't happy when his shoulder was shaken in the morning. His mother was standing beside the bed, a cup of tea on the bedside table. With one eye, he looked at the clock.

"Eight o'clock! I said I didn't want to be awakened for anything," he growled at her.

"Sit up and drink your tea. There are things to be done."

"Oh God! Has that bloody dog bitten the postman again?" he asked bitterly but sat up.

Somewhat to his surprise—they weren't normally a demonstrative couple—Ella bent down and kissed him.

"Happy birthday, Richard," she said.

"What the devil are you on about? I haven't been asleep for three months!"

"You'll think it's your birthday, though. The Post Office has just rung through to say a cable arrived for you. Kate will be at Heathrow about four o'clock this afternoon."

Richard looked at her, incredulously and then he let out one tremendous shout of joy, threw back the bedclothes, and leapt out of bed.

Ella covered her eyes in mock horror for he was as naked as the day he was born, too tired last night to fumble around for his pajamas. He wrapped a dressing gown around himself, hugged his mother, and fell back on the bed. "I don't believe it!" he said.

"Please yourself!" Ella retorted, almost as happy as her son. "But there are a thousand things to be done. I've got to pack for one thing and be away from here before you go to the airport. I take it you'll be meeting her even though you don't believe it."

"Oh, Mum," he protested, but half-heartedly. "There's no need for you to go today, you know."

"Nonsense!" came the firm reply. "You'll want Kate and the house to yourself. Come and see me when you feel like it, but Fuzz and I are off. Don't feel guilty, boy. I wouldn't want anybody around if it was me. I quite understand, so stop being silly."

* * * *

The morning flashed past. Richard was in tremendous spirits, looking at his watch about every ten minutes.

Ella told him she was glad to see his happiness and yet, sad at the thought of leaving. "Never mind," she said. "I've got Fuzz now to keep me company."

While they were pretending to eat lunch, he tried to thank her for all she'd done, but being Richard he put it in a different way.

"Now listen to me, mother. All this business with the ladies has given me a lot to think about and particularly about you. I'd like you to sell the flat and come down here a bit nearer to us. Wait a sec..." as she was going to butt in. "...it's what I want, and I always get my own way, don't I? Kate and you get along well together. In fact, she suggested something of the sort when we found this house, and after the events of the past week or so, I'm determined. So we'll start looking around for a suitable place for you and that twopenn'orth of cats' meat. Subject closed!"

Richard was at Heathrow far too early and spent the waiting time convinced the plane would crash, or she wouldn't be on it. But in it flew and after a short delay, there she was, his darling Kate. She had no baggage except her handbag and a large holdall which she'd taken on the plane with her.

She was radiant and tanned and happy. He shoved everybody aside to reach her and without a word took her in his arms, oblivious to everything else in the world. How long they stood like that could have been minutes or hours, but they parted with reluctance. Richard's first words, apart from a few incoherent endearments, were prosaic.

"Where's the rest of your luggage, darling?"

"There isn't any," she said. "I was in such a hurry to get back to you. I've left it all behind. Doesn't matter. They'll send it on. Only clothes, anyway."

With his arm tightly around her in case she vanished from his sight, Richard took her out to the car, turned to kiss her again, and said, "Home, my darling Kate. Our own home."

As he negotiated his way out of the airport, Kate asked about Ella and was told she'd gone to her own home and why.

"A very wise lady, your mother," Kate said, her hand tucked comfortably in the crook of his arm as he drove. Then they both suddenly fell silent as if a shyness had descended on them, but it was a loving and companionable silence. There would be plenty of time for words later.

Presently, when they were fairly clear of traffic, Kate

said, "Pull onto the side of the road, please, darling."

Richard shot a worried glance at her. Was she feeling carsick after the long journey? He pulled in and faced her, looking anxious. "What is it? Are you all right?"

"It's no good!" she said. "I can't possibly wait until we get home to tell you. And I'd got it all planned to the last detail how I was going to break the news."

Richard was terrified out of his wits. "What news?" he managed to get out of a dry mouth.

"That we're going to have a baby," his miraculous Kate told him.

A moment of stunned silence and then a giant roar from Richard which nearly stopped the traffic. What they both said, both talking together, was entirely satisfactory to themselves, and it was a good ten minutes before he moved off.

"When?" he wanted to know and "why didn't you write and tell me?"

"I'm three months pregnant, so work it out for yourself. And how could I have written something as important as this? You'd have come roaring over as soon as you heard. Did you notice how short my letters to you were getting? I couldn't make them any longer for fear I'd blurt it all out."

Richard laughed. "Did I notice! I thought you'd found some handsome New Zealander. I thought you'd got tired of me, I thought you'd decided you wanted to stay in your old home, I thought—oh, God knows what I've been thinking. Mother's been giving me a hard time because I was getting so crotchety. Mother! Can you imagine, darling, what she's going to say when she hears our news? That'll settle her hash now. She'll have to move nearer. We'll need her to babysit when I take you out and

234

show you off to all the new friends I've been making."

"Dearest idiot! I hope to be meeting people before then. The baby isn't arriving tomorrow."

"I'm entitled to be as much of an idiot as I like." And he began to sing.

He sobered down before they reached Burshill and asked so many questions that in the end, Kate rebelled.

"I hope you won't turn into one of those stupid fathers-to-be who think I should be wrapped in cotton wool from now on. I won't have it. Let's talk about our baby. I've decided you can choose the name if it's a boy, and I'll choose if it's a girl. Okay?"

Richard would have agreed to anything in his euphoric state but...

"What do you want her called? But it's going to be a boy! However, if you fall down on the job, and it's a girl, I'll try to bear up. So what will her name be?"

"Laura!" his wife replied.

He nearly turned the car around and drove his darling Kate back to Heathrow!

Majorie Grace Patricia Bridget Owen

About the Author

Marjorie Grace Patricia Bridget Owen was born on September 11th 1911 in England and endured the bombardment of World War II. As far as we know, she was born out-of-wedlock with an Irish Lord for a father and a Russian princess as her mother. Although her life before working is somewhat sketchy, her career, as a major London department store clothing buyer, was long and interesting. Members of the Royal family were amongst some of her more famous clients.

Marjorie found time to write many short stories and four novels ranging from romance to mystery. She did not attempt to publish any of her writings. We can only surmise that she wrote for the joy and did not wish to seek any recognition or fame.

Marjorie lived in the town of Burgess Hill in the county of Sussex, England referred to in the book as Burshill. The first murder took place in what could well have been St. Johns Park. This was an area in front of the apartment, above the local Post Office, in which she lived for many years.

She had no hot water in the apartment and had to wash herself in the ground floor kitchen before the Post Office staff arrived for work. With no heating, she relied on a coal fire to keep warm in the cold and drafty winter months. This forced her to carry buckets of coal up the stairs until her son, daughter-in-law, and grandchildren talked her into moving to an assisted living facility in the same town.

The town of Burgess Hill dates back to 1342 and a Roman road passed through the town as a link from London, in the north, to Brighton and Hove on the south coast. There is no evidence that the Romans spent any time in Burgess Hill.

When Marjorie worked in department stores in London, she would walk to the railway station and catch a train to Victoria Station. She did this in all weathers and the road she walked was sometimes covered in snow.

She actually changed her birth certificate from 1911 to 1917 so that she could continue to work for an additional six years after her retirement age of 60.

After a very full life, Marjorie passed away on March 28th 2004, at the age of ninety-three.

A brief history of Burgess Hill

 Burgess Hill has developed from the northern parts of Clayton and Keymer parishes with later additions from Ditchling, Hurstpierpoint and Wivesfielfd. It grew from an area of common grazing land known as St. John's Common, the name being taken from a sheep and lamb fair held on St. John the Baptist day and dates back to 1342. It was held in the northwest corner of the Common known as Fairplace.

There were thirty-two farmhouses around the Common before 1950, but only eight now remain. Schools were later established for the growing population. Hotels were opened, catering for visitors who found it beneficial to take advantage of the town's amenities and tranquility. Part of the Martlets shopping precinct was once a tree-lined road, with large houses built in times of Victorian prosperity.

Large pleasure gardens opened in 1897 by local farmer and butcher Mr. Edwin Street to celebrate Queen Victoria's Diamond Jubilee. The "Victoria Pleasure Gardens" contained a large lake covering three acres, used for boating and skating in the winter. It is now the site of Victoria Industrial Estate.

From the sixteenth century a number of brickworks and potteries flourished, sending products far a field after the railways came in the 1840s. For 100 years from 1830 to 1930, three-quarters of Burgess Hill were predominantly brick, tile, and pottery making works.

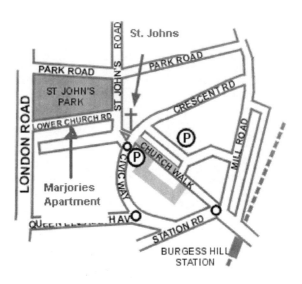

If you liked Ladies of Class you might enjoy the following mystery romance available now from Vintage Romance Publishing:

Dead on the Money
Venita Louise
ISBN: 0-9793327-2-9
Mystery/light romance
Trade Paperback: $13.95

Dead on the Money, picks up where Initials For Murder, left off, ensnaring Tom and Olivia in yet another dangerous and thrilling adventure.

Tom Trask is basking in the glow of his recent engagement to H. Olivia Tully, but without warning, his elation turns to shattering danger when a ruthless convict shows up and begins to stalk them.

Reviews

"Venita Louise is dead on the money with her descriptive scenes, mannerisms, and even her fashion sense, giving readers a peek in to the past." Fallen Angel Reviews

"I haven't had this satisfying a laugh in a LONG time. Thanks Ms. Louise, you are a pearl. Please write more! I can't wait for the next book!"- Hazelstreet Productions

"The characters are supremely drawn and come to life like real and three-dimensional persons." -Euro Reviews

"This gal is a real pro and it shows. Her material is top drawer throughout..."-Bob Mills, former writer for Bob Hope

Available now from all major online retailers and your favorite bookstore.

Majorie Grace Patricia Bridget Owen

Printed in the United States
201176BV00001B/7-15/P

9 780979 332753